# PENGUIN METRO READS
## TELL ME A STORY

Ravinder Singh is the bestselling author of *I Too Had a Love Story*, *Can Love Happen Twice?*, *Like It Happened Yesterday*, *Your Dreams Are Mine Now* and *This Love That Feels Right . . .* After having spent most of his life in Burla, a small town in western Odisha, Ravinder is currently based in New Delhi. He has an MBA from the renowned Indian School of Business. His eight-year-long IT career started with Infosys and came to a happy ending at Microsoft where he worked as a senior programme manager. One fine day he had an epiphany that writing books is more interesting than writing project plans. He called it a day at work and took to full-time writing. He has also started a venture called Black Ink (www.BlackInkBooks.in) to publish debut authors. Ravinder loves playing snooker in his free time. He is also crazy about Punjabi music and enjoys dancing to its beats.

You can reach out to him on his Twitter handle: @RavinderSingh.

# Tell Me a Story

EDITED BY

# RAVINDER SINGH

PENGUIN
metro reads

An imprint of Penguin Random House

PENGUIN METRO READS

USA | Canada | UK | Ireland | Australia
New Zealand | India | South Africa | China

Penguin Metro Reads is part of the Penguin Random House group of companies
whose addresses can be found at global.penguinrandomhouse.com

Published by Penguin Random House India Pvt. Ltd
7th Floor, Infinity Tower C, DLF Cyber City,
Gurgaon 122 002, Haryana, India

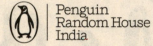
Penguin
Random House
India

First published in Penguin Metro Reads by Penguin Books India 2015

Anthology copyright © Penguin Books India 2015
Editor's note copyright © Ravinder Singh 2015
The copyright for individual pieces vests with the authors or their estates

All rights reserved

14 13 12 11 10 9

This is a work of fiction. Names, characters, places and incidents are either the
product of the authors' imagination or are used fictitiously and any resemblance
to any actual person, living or dead, events or locales is entirely coincidental.

ISBN 9780143423010

Typeset in Bembo Pro by Manipal Digital Systems, Manipal
Printed at Thomson Press India Ltd, New Delhi

BRENT LIBRARIES

EAL

91120000350340

| Askews & Holts | 29-Nov-2017 |
| AF | £7.99 |
|  |  |

This b... ...subject to the condition that it shall not, by way of trade
or oth... ...thout the
publis... ...an that in
which ... ...s condition

# Contents

# *Editor's Note*

We all have stories to tell. And we love telling them, don't we? That's what we do almost every day—in college canteens, on the cab ride to office, over the phone, on WhatsApp and a lot more on social networking websites. We *do* spend a lot of time telling stories!

Sometimes they are lengthy and we break them into paragraphs, sometimes we limit them to a mere 140 characters. They are stories that we pour out of ourselves with the idea that others will read or hear them with the same excitement and interest as we tell or write them.

But then there is that one story which is so close to your heart, that hell of a story that touches you like no other every time you recall it. On some idle Saturday night you laugh, reliving that story for one more time. And at that exact moment, someone far away from you sheds tears, remembering her story for one more time. One thing is for sure—these are your real life stories. They are so powerful that they move you every time you go back in the past and relive them. They are your lowest lows and your highest highs. They are the lows that have helped you to aspire for the highest. Then there are those that have changed you as a person; those that have changed your idea of the people involved—but they are not inconsequential or insignificant. Because the changes they have brought about are not small. You still remember them, share them.

Having already narrated stories from my life, I wanted my readers to tell me incidents from theirs that deeply changed them. And why is that? Well, many of you have been writing to me anyway. You have been sharing with me your life stories over emails, private messages and on my social networking pages. Isn't it great that we are sharing these stories with the world, with people who might have had similar experiences? I wanted to provide a platform that is not private any more. I wanted to compile these life experiences in an anthology that is like an album of memories.

So I asked people to 'Tell Me a Story', from their own lives or from the lives of people who are around them. And I promised them that the ones that touched my heart the most would find a place in this anthology that you are holding in your hands. I must say, it was a difficult task for me and my team at Penguin Random House to go through the large number of submissions we received. The beauty of this project was that we read about people's lives. We laughed, we cried and we identified with the stories as we read them. We debated and discussed what worked, what didn't. But we all agreed that it was marvellous how the contestants had opened up their hearts to narrate to us that one most important story from their lives.

And then I arrived at these twenty-one innocent, heart-touching, heart-warming, soul-stirring stories that are so different from each other and at the same time so alike. They are different in terms of their plot, their characters and their narrations. But they are alike in terms of the gravity of the emotions they hold. Some will make you happy. Some will make you sad. Like they did us. But I believe that when you read them, you will connect with them. And when you do so, they may make you recall your story—that one hell of an episode from your life which you would want to share with the world, before your time is over.

Just remember, if you undergo this very urge, while you are on your journey to reading these twenty-one beautiful stories, I wholeheartedly invite you, too, to *Tell Me a Story* . . .

Ravinder Singh

# The End of the Tunnel

KRISHNASISH JANA

Honestly, I had never imagined I would be opening this leaf from the book of my life ever again. It was presumably buried deep beneath the thick misty veils of what everybody calls 'memory'. But there are some incidents that, at the sudden mention of certain words, shoot back as colourful kaleidoscopes right before your eyes, and then change, very slowly, to calm and clear images. The images I saw were not so clear, but for a moment I could smell the strange aura of grievance around me, which was an extraordinary case of déjà vu. *The smell brought me tears.*

I was a fourteen-year-old kid then, and I barely knew anything other than my parents, my home, my school, and the 'ice-cream man' at the gate. It was just another dull afternoon. My school van halted by the lane to my house, and I sprinted towards the newly painted gate, and saw my mother waiting for me. I opened the gate, but she hardly noticed the sound. That was something I experienced for the first time in my life. She could never have been so preoccupied. *What was that she was so deeply absorbed in?* For a moment I stared at her blankly, and the next moment, it struck me like a massive lightning bolt. I walked towards her. She suddenly turned around. Her eyes were swollen. I managed to ask, 'Is it about Uncle?'

She did not reply. But I saw the terrible confirmation of my fears trickle as a callous teardrop down her cheek.

*So, it's over. He's gone. Forever . . .*

She took my bag from me, offered me a dry smile, and said, 'Come upstairs, your lunch is ready.'

I did not ask any more questions. As I entered the house, I felt a weird silence all around. Even the leaves of the trees seemed to hustle with utmost caution. I tried to have a peek into my grandmother's room, but my mother pulled me up the stairs. My father was nowhere to be seen.

I had my bath. I was not very surprised, because I had actually been praying to God for this. When the imminence of death stares right into one's helpless eyes, it's better to leave early than to stay a little longer and bear more pain quite unnecessarily. My uncle's cancer was terminal. He never touched a cigarette in his life, and yet it was lung cancer.

*Fate really knows how to mock itself at times.*

I wasn't allowed to visit him in the hospital. 'He's no longer the uncle you know,' was the rational answer that was supposed to satiate my uncontrollable curiosity. But from their conversations I realized very well that my uncle was going through a lot of pain, unavoidable pain perhaps, while we all knew what the end would exactly be. I was too naïve to understand that the weakness of consanguinity was the only solid justification. Hope was everything then. Everything.

*And now he was gone.*

I ate quietly, and so did my mother. When I was going to bed for my regular afternoon nap, I mustered courage and asked her, 'Where's Father?'

'He is returning from the hospital. They are bringing back your . . .' she paused and paraphrased, '. . . the body.'

I did not know what to say. *He would be ashes by evening. And yet I can hear his voice, fresh and alive, still ringing in my ears . . . calling out my name, with one hand behind him, hiding a story book, for me . . .*

After a few hours, I heard a couple of cars screeching to a halt at our gate. But what I heard next shall always keep reverberating in the corridors of our house—I heard a mother howl helplessly, calling out the name of her son who would never respond. I rushed down and watched my uncle covered in a stretch of white cloth, and my grandmother screaming and trying to shake him up furiously. It looked like a big pot of suppressed sorrow had suddenly burst open.

I had seen this scene a hundred times in movies and TV serials. But seeing this right before my own eyes, with my own family members instead of unknown faces, was a horrible experience. I could feel my mother's grip tighten around my wrist. She was crying, and it was no longer under her control. 'Come back! You don't have to see this!' She kept on pleading, but I did not budge. *I had to see.*

My grandmother was gradually slowing down. Her shadow seemed to relentlessly pull her back on the ground, whispering in her ears that no matter how much she shouted, her son was too far to hear her. Her swollen eyes seemed ready to close any moment, because of the tempestuous deluge they had been suffering. She slowly stopped thumping on her dead son's chest. Gradually, her voice lost its intensity.

She placed her head on the wooden cot. My aunts and my father carried her slowly back to her room. She had lost all her energy to resist.

Neighbours had already gathered all around. The look on their faces made me think that it was the first time someone had died in this world. No one cared to offer us any privacy. And for me, this was the first death in my life till then . . . the first *untimely* death, I mean. I had not noticed that I had been crying too. In fact, quite furiously so. I wiped my tears and looked at the cold lifeless fingers of my uncle that were peeking out from under the white cloth. I watched my didi, my uncle's daughter, gazing blankly at her father, as if she was seeing something that was impossible to believe. She had not uttered a word, nor did she shed a single tear. All she did was stand, like a mannequin, and watch her father. Someone had sucked all her life out of her in one terrible moment. All that was left of her was her silhouette. Her mother was sitting at her feet. She was continuously muttering something. I tried to imagine my cousin's position, and trembled at the thought. I remember I had silently prayed for her.

That evening my uncle was cremated. My father came back. I felt sorry for him. He talked to nobody. He took a bath, and cleansed his belongings with *Gangajal* as was customary. I was sitting idle, looking out of the window. My mother came and sat beside me.

'Mother, one day we all shall die.'

'We will, my child,' she said and smiled. 'Now try to forget this . . .'

'Can you promise me one thing?'

She looked at me. I continued, 'You and father won't leave me when I'm still alive, because I won't be able to bear this. Whenever we go, we go together. Nobody has to grieve.'

For a few seconds she kept gaping at me, trying to understand what exactly I had been pondering over. She then somehow gathered herself and said, 'Death does not give anyone choice or time, child.' She hugged me warmly and said, 'But we can fight death for you. I promise.'

A sudden shade of relief ran across my face. She said again, 'This place we live in, it isn't nice at all, son. Your uncle has left an ugly place and is on his way to a much more beautiful and serene one. He will be flying with the birds, dancing with the flowers, shining amongst the stars . . . He has just completed a long tiresome journey. Let him rest now.'

I looked at her and asked her, 'Can I go and meet her?'

She knew who I was referring to. She nodded.

I slowly walked down to my grandmother's room and watched her sitting like a stone statue looking at the lazy rotation of the fan blades. The lamp in the small wooden temple was still unlit. The gods were smiling in the dark. I crawled up to her bed and sat beside her. She had drifted away to some place far from this world it seemed. She mumbled to herself after a few minutes, 'Why doesn't He take me? So many years I have lived. I have seen enough. Isn't it time for me to leave? What more does He want me to see?'

She looked at me. She was broken to the last bit. Her voice was reduced to a whisper filled with tremors. I knew if anybody found me sitting with her, I would be pulled out immediately. But I wanted her to talk to someone. It did not matter whether that someone was a fourteen-year-old.

'Grandma, isn't it better now? All those medicines, painful injections, dreadful treatments . . . all that is over. No hope does any good if it's constantly fluctuating, Grandma. He is at peace now . . .'

'How do we know?' She actually said this a little louder. 'No one knows what happens after death! Maybe he's just walking now . . . walking, without pause . . . with no light on the other side of the tunnel . . . maybe he's still calling out for me.'

I never meant to say anything that would tease out her tears instead of easing her heart. I was a child, and I did not realize that the heart of a mother who has lost her child cannot be *eased* by any means possible. Truly, what do we know of death? Is it just an end? Or is there more after the end?

I tried to say something meaningful, and decided to stick to my mother's words.

'Grandma, he has just completed a long tiresome journey. Let him rest now.'

My grandmother looked right into my eyes. It was a strange look, something that had left an indelible picture registered in my mind. Her eyes showed a collage of myriad emotions. A soft smile slowly quivered on her trembling lips, and she hugged me tightly before bursting into tears again. 'He will be at peace . . .' she whispered.

I replied, 'He will be. He will be.'

After that day, I had found my grandmother weeping secretly on numerous occasions. Many a times I had noticed her staring at the framed photograph on the wall, as if awaiting answers. But every time she looked away, there was no sign of unrest in her eyes. Instead, there was an unnaturally calm and peaceful gaze. She knew she would never see her son walking towards her with a smile, but somewhere deep within she believed he was indeed smiling, and watching her. She was free from the unbearable suffering that she had gone through, watching her son turn into a skeleton because of medications. She knew all the pain had ended.

Adhering to the Almighty's decree is the only option that's left with us, and by 'us' I mean 'humans'. Death has no explanation, no aftermath. It's just the end of a long tiresome journey. But what we choose to see more brightly is that it is also the beginning of a long endless rest. Finding positivity in something as dark as death is perhaps the biggest inspiration a human being can achieve. Why do we fear darkness? Why can we not carry lights? Instead of fearing death, we should fear wasting a life for nothing. The end should not be on a bed full of regrets, with a bunch of people crying, and if you are rich, a big device by your side showing you your own heart rate gradually ceasing to a halt. It must be a moment of the most peaceful smile and the heaviest sigh of relief.

I had learnt a lesson that evening. If you have come, you have to go. And when you have to go, live your life in such a manner that you are even more present in your absence. That's achievement. That's true inspiration. Even if the death is untimely, be a good human being the days you have been clinging on to. Find a place in the hearts of not only your loved ones, but everyone you know, for that place shall never be granted to anybody else.

Because it is only death that can inspire life like nothing else.

# The Smile That Said It All

## KAMALIKA RAY

It was a freezing night in the middle of December. The complete darkness was only broken occasionally by little man-made bonfires near sleeping beggars on cold barren roads. The last liquor shops were being shut by shaky hands.

Nearly twenty years back.

Time: Around 10 o'clock at night.

Place: Ranchi.

A chilly wind was howling outside, angry that all doors and openings were closed to it. Trees swayed to it, as if dancing, to calm it down.

My mother had made sure that my sister and I locked all the windows before we sat for our routine after-dinner study. Papa had gone for his monthly business tour, and Ma, as usual, took extra precautions for our safety, by checking and rechecking every latch. There had been a robbery in the neighbourhood recently, which had left every one of us suspicious of even our own shadows, especially in these kinds of eerie nights.

It was a blessing though, that our society mostly housed our relatives, and the newly appointed watchman, Mohan Gurung, was known to Papa.

In those days, like most small cities, electricity in Ranchi was a big problem (it still is, in a few parts). Frequent loadshedding, intolerable voltage fluctuations were almost a daily routine. Bursting bulbs, burnt fuses were normal; it was more frustrating than anything else. But sometimes, it proved to be a boon for sleepy kids like us, tired of studying at night, waiting to snuggle into our warm beds.

So I was secretly quite happy when all of a sudden the lights went off that night. It did feel a bit strange since, for the past few months, there hadn't been a single power cut at this hour! The emergency light charger had gone for repairing and with all the windows closed, curtains drawn, in a second it was pitch dark all around.

Taken aback by the suddenness, the three of us did not move for a minute, moaning and groaning. Then, all three of us gathered together, formed a chain by holding hands and went about rummaging in the sitting room for a torch or a candle in the dark. Thanks to my dear sister, things were never kept back in place. Finally, my hands touched wax . . . and yes! a candle! But it is perhaps nature's law that when you find a candle, you will almost never find a matchbox nearby. Our chain had to grope our way back to the kitchen, to turn the gas on to light the candle. As the little flicker of fire appeared, killing the dark in a single flash, we finally smiled, at each other—victorious and relieved. It was then that all three of us . . . heard the knock.

Rap. Rap. Rap.

Thrice.

Silence.

Then again . . . Rap. Rap. Rap!

Someone was knocking on the main door. Softly . . . firmly . . . a bit urgently.

Drained out of all emotions, in disbelief, the three of us stood riveted to our spots. Our eyes wide open, looking at each other, flickered with the reflection of the flame of the candle Ma held . . . or was it fear?

Who could it be there at this hour? What was that idiot watchman doing? He must have missed this intruder's entry! Now what do we do?

'Surely burglars won't come knocking on the main door, will they?' Ma tried to smile at us.

But her expression confused me. Was she giving us assurance or asking for it?

RAP!

A knock again. This time, a bit louder, impatient.

Without a warning, my sister suddenly cried out . . . 'Who is it?'

Though angry at her suddenness, Ma and I both waited to listen. A minute passed, but there was just silence.

Then again a knock.

Instead of going to the door, my mother rushed to our guest room to call out to the watchman. Thank God, we were on the ground floor, and the watchman's room was within audible distance from that room.

With the single candle gone, again in the dark, we sisters tiptoed our way to the main door and I glued my eyes to the eyehole. As expected, nothing was visible. But slowly, my eyes adjusted, and then, I saw her.

An apparition, silhouetted against a bright torchlight coming from behind her. Our watchman, Mohan, was rushing towards our house. Hurriedly, Ma shoved me behind her, and opened the door, with the safety chain latched in place.

Mohan Gurung was shouting at a crouching figure in the dark.

'*Kaun hain tu? Kaise ghus aayi idhar?*' (Who are you? How did you enter?)

My mother was standing at our door, watching carefully. My sister and I were struggling for a good view from behind her.

The apparition was a woman, young or old, I could not tell. The watchman's ragged lantern didn't help much. She was an adivasi, dark-skinned, very thin and very frightened. Seeing her nervous, somewhere within, we felt at ease. And we came out a little to look at her. Her sari, torn at places, soiled and dirty beyond description, did little to cover her bare, shivering body. Still, a tiny pallu had managed to cover her head, which she kept lowered as she sat huddled up near the end of the stairs, below our meter board. She looked filthy, and her stench was nearly unbearable. How many days had she not bathed?

Mohan was shouting at her non-stop . . . making the most of an opportunity to prove his efficiency. She kept shrinking into herself as his decibels increased. I could hear doors being opened upstairs.

'*Kaun ho, behen?*' Ma finally had found her voice and managed to ask who she was.

Slowly, in response, she looked up towards us, her face astonishingly young, eyes full of fear, anticipation, and pain.

'Roti . . .' the voice was cracked, dry, tired.

She dropped her head into her folded knees. Hugging herself more tightly, as if that would help her fight the cold.

'The brown warm blanket on our bed. Quick!' Ma's order to my sister was almost instant.

Sharma Chacha had come down, after carefully putting on, I noticed, all the woollens he had ever owned it seemed, taking updates from Mohan. He then raised his big lantern to see her clearly. She cringed back in the light, trying to cover herself and failing, but not trying to get up, at all.

'Informers! Spies! People like these! Nothing else!' Sharma Chacha declared, 'Get her out of this place this minute! Who knows, a gang might be following her! Just inform the police!'

The blanket had come, but the recipient was too scared to take it now. Her hands were shaking miserably. Her tear-stained face showed she wanted to say something, but all that came out were short dry coughs.

The stench around her was awful . . . and I had to stop breathing to go near her to throw the blanket towards her.

Sudden warmth, sudden comfort, sudden love, is just as unbelievable at first, as sudden pain.

As carefully, slowly, she started to pull the blanket towards herself, Sharma Chachi, who had finally found the courage to come down, bellowed at Ma, 'Why all this, Rama? Let's just throw her out!'

A couple of more families had come down, mutely watching, with lit torches in hands, their nervous faces safely hidden in the dark.

'Not without some food in her stomach, Didi, she came knocking at MY door.'

I was amazed at my Ma's calmness. Wow. I had never seen my mother like this before! And I definitely loved what I saw.

The watchman, Sharma Chacha, Sharma Chachi, and the few 'men' whose curiosity had won over their fright, stood there with torches, lanterns in hand, huddled together, at a safe distance, watching her, commenting on the futility of

Ma's actions, of the grave dangers that lay ahead if we let the woman stay any longer.

The hapless creature kept her head as lowered as possible, not once looking up, as if, if she couldn't see them, they couldn't see her too. But she was visible, under scrutiny, under their flashlights and lanterns, her scabbed hands and feet were being focused on by lit torches. Her dry straw-like flowing hair, her whole reeking body was being commented upon, and what's more, people were even looking for signs of her being married or not.

It was, as if, she was a stray animal, and definitely not a woman.

Her shivering body, her visible discomfort at being scrutinized by so many unknown men, didn't get anybody's sympathy. Not even from the women standing there.

Outside, we calculated, the temperature must have dipped to about 2–3 degrees.

Inside, I realized, our hearts were more frozen than our chilled hands.

The air was heavy with agitated emotions, when Ma re-entered the scene. 'My own Florence Nightingale,' I couldn't help thinking, complete with a candle in one hand, and food in the other. Ignoring the sarcasm-filled mumbles, Ma handed her the rotis and a bowl of hot milk.

The food, at last, did the trick.

Tears trickled down as in a broken voice, in between coarse coughs, she told us her story . . .

Her village was near Khunti. Her husband had thrown her out some time back, for another woman. With no one other than an old, blind mother in a remote village, she had no option but to take refuge forcibly with a relative in Ranchi. A few days back, she got thrown out a second time. She had been roaming on the roads ever since.

Sharma Chacha was impatient. They couldn't make out clearly what the woman was saying to my mother. They were cold, irritated, waiting to get back to their warm beds. What was taking this woman so long?

'What if she goes tomorrow morning?' As soon as the words came out of my mother's mouth, an avalanche of heated arguments poured down outrageously. Had my mother lost her senses? The men were muttering angrily in their breaths . . . cursing Papa's absence.

All of a sudden, a clear male voice came from upstairs, 'Why don't you send her to Nirmal Hriday? It's not that far away . . .' It was Yadav's paying guest speaking.

Bingo!

Whenever a good idea comes, or a good solution to a grave problem, its ownership is always disputed over, claimed for. Many said they were thinking the same thing. Some, too proud to admit defeat, said, 'Think again.' But in a subtle way, everyone had instantly liked and accepted the proposition. Yes, it satisfied both, their need, and their conscience, if any.

Only Ma was still unsure. She called Sharma Chachi and said something I could not hear. But I saw Chachi cringe and wrinkle her nose as she looked at the woman from head to toe. Her look had more disdain than before.

I finally understood minutes later when the woman had to finally get up. The portion of the sari behind her was almost blackened by old blood marks. The poor woman, to top all her miseries, had been menstruating. She had been unwilling to stand, all this while, for this very reason.

Mohan had been sent some time back to catch a cycle rickshaw. He could be heard stopping and trying to convince the passing rickshaws.

As we all waited with bated breath, Ma finally did her last act of humanity by giving her an old sari.

Sharma Chachi's huge fat figure at last found a use, when the woman, uncomfortable in the presence of so many staring men, hastily wrapped the sari around herself in the shadow of Chachi.

A cycle rickshaw had come, honking needlessly to announce its arrival. Mohan gave directions at the top of his voice, too excited to be of some use finally. The paying guest of Yadav's had come down. 'We shouldn't send her alone at this hour. It's not safe.' The other men around grumbled inside their breaths. 'Now what next?'

Ultimately, there was some display of benevolence when they instructed Mohan to accompany her to Nirmal Hriday, Mother Teresa's home for destitutes, a thirty-minute ride from our home.

It was almost midnight when the rickshaw finally pulled out of our gate. Quite characteristically, Mohan, with his fingers clutching his nose, had made the woman sit on the floor, like an untouchable.

She had obediently followed whatever they said, nodding her lowered head lightly when being told particularly to feel grateful, how kind everybody was being to her. But when she left, before climbing onto the rickshaw, the single time she had lifted her face, her eyes had only and only gazed at my mother, and nobody else. I was too young to read eyes at that time, but I guess, she wanted to say, 'Thank you.'

As days passed, we all completely forgot about the woman. We just proudly remembered our own 'act of kindness'. It didn't really matter that Mohan had merely dumped her in front of the closed gates of Nirmal Hriday that night and turned around immediately. What only mattered was that we were kind enough not to have handed her over to the police. We were all good people, after all.

Like the seasons of nature, which wait for none, time too flows in its own pace, in its own space.

It was months after that night, when God put her in front of us, again.

It was a Friday evening, Ma and I had gone to buy vegetables at the market. As we strolled on with half-empty bags, checking on vegetables, someone called from behind.

'Didi!'

To our surprise, a young adivasi woman, smiling widely, was standing on the road, and calling to my mother!

At first we ignored her and turned back, but she called again!

This time, she came running to us!

'*Nahi pehchaane na, Didi* (You didn't recognize me)?' she asked with a smile.

'I came to your house that night, Didi? You gave me roti? Remember?'

As our minds reeled back in astonishment, I couldn't help noticing how beautiful she looked now!

She was wearing a colourful printed synthetic sari, long earrings, a large bindi on her forehead, and an ear-to-ear smile dimming out the rest.

'I stayed with the sisters in Nirmal Hriday . . . then I moved out. They helped me start earning. I come here weekly, Didi. I sell ladies' items, mirrors, combs, jewellery . . . many more things! You want something, Didi? I will give you for free!'

We didn't know what to say, all of a sudden, ashamed at our past ignorance, at the display of such gratefulness.

'What about your husband?' Ma was at a loss for words, too, it seemed.

'I don't know where he is. I don't care now. I have to go, Didi.' She had left her place on the road unguarded.

So many questions were bubbling up inside us, as we saw her crossing the busy road with amazing ease. Where did she stay now? Was she earning well enough? Was she well? Was she happy?

But all we saw was her smile when she turned around to see us again, a wide, toothy smile.

And that smile said it all.

# The Defender

## APARAJITA DUTTA

'You can't play football any more,' the doctor announced in a very grave tone as he carefully examined the X-ray reports. Clearly aware of what was going on in Labdhyo's mind, I dared not look at him. I expected an outburst, but strangely, silence was all I could hear. My eyes were blurred by the dates of the upcoming tournaments, inter-hostel and inter-departmental, and my eardrums seemed to break by the cheering of the words, 'Captain Labdhyo!'

'You should see the physiotherapist soon.' The doctor's voice broke the silence. 'Take the medicines, painkillers, when you need them. Remember, a slipped disc is not a joke.'

*What was happening to me?* I wondered. Had I become deaf? Was I too scared to hear the cry of a heartbroken man, for whom football meant everything? Was I scared to hear the syllables of anguish from a man who had played football at u-17 levels for his district but could not take up the game as a profession because of career constraints and his strong principle of not polluting his love and passion by making it a way to gain financial stability? I have seen Labdhyo play since our college days at Jadavpur University. Known as Neuer among his friends, he had been one of the most valued players of the football group FIIOB (Football Is in Our Blood) and has been captaining the Chemical Engineering Department team of IIT KGP where he was pursuing a PhD. Apart from that he was also the captain of the Nehru Hall Football Team. Football has always been his first love and at twenty-eight, he had no plans to retire.

'Thank you,' came the familiar voice I was waiting for. Labdhyo gingerly got off the bed, taking the prescription. I reached out to collect the biometry reports.

'What time is it aJd?' he asked me calling by my nickname as we walked out of the IIT KGP Medical Centre. 'I left my phone at the lab.'

'Four o'clock,' I said checking my watch. I had not been able to gather my strength and ask about his decisions.

'Great. Match starts at five.'

He left me baffled. I was not sure what to do, I was not aware of his intentions. Did he wish to inform his team that he couldn't play and help them choose another goalkeeper? Or . . .

'Could you call Nil and ask him to bring my bag directly to the field?' Labdhyo continued to interrupt my flow of thoughts.

'Umm, which bag?' I asked, still doubtful about his intentions.

'The one where I have my gloves, shin guards, socks, and other stuff,' he replied. 'Want to grab a cold coffee from Sahara?'

I anticipated this was coming.

'So you will play?' I finally managed to ask.

'Yes, why not?' he reacted as if I had asked something bizarre.

'Labdhyo . . . but the doctor . . .'

'Who gave you the project at the English Department here? I will sue him for bringing in a nagging parrot from Kolkata.'

'Just a matter of few months,' I grumbled. Labdhyo and I had been pretty good friends but he would never pay any heed to my repeated utterings of, 'Please try to take care of yourself.'

'Machoism,' I muttered under my breath. Labdhyo pretended to not hear.

Sipping on my cold coffee at Sahara, I said, 'You have injured your shin, Neuer. You really think you can play for Ruud Shock?'

'Cazzz,' Labdhyo yawned, as if nothing has happened.

'You and your cazzz,' I said to myself, cursing this short form of the word 'casual' which Labdhyo would perhaps use even while he was dying.

'You have your departmental game on Friday and we have to be there at Kolkata for Saturday morning's match.' I tried my best to convince him.

'Tell Rweeto to bring my jersey.'

'What?' I was shocked. 'You will play for the FIIOB Winter Shield too?'

'I have to rush for the game. Come if you want.' Labdhyo walked out leaving a fifty-rupee note on the bill. I collected the change after a tip and dragged myself to the ground. Throughout the match, I pondered over my responsibility as one of the managers of Labdhyo's team of the FIIOB: Ruud Shock. We had just a few days left in our hands, and after rounds of auctions, we had very little money left to buy another keeper. Knowing about his health condition, I didn't want Labdhyo to play, from the deepest core of my heart. But I was left with no option.

'Don't you dare to mope over what happened today,' Labdhyo warned me as we were returning from practice. 'I will play all the games.' I walked along silently and left him earlier than usual.

I was unusually silent on the days that followed for I was torn between friendship and duty. I knew every move Labdhyo was making was detrimental to his health. But what could be done? The game must go on. Friday's victory in the departmental tournament lifted up our spirits as we travelled back to Kolkata for the tourney. I, the only female manager in the twelve teams, was of course excited.

Saturday, however, proved fatal for us. With more than four players injured and a very weak defence, we lost the matches. Labdhyo was perhaps the only one in the team who stayed on the ground throughout, without complaining.

As promised to him, I didn't talk about his injury or his degrading health condition but kept a spray with me, which he used often—most of the time actually.

'I feel a little odd to use the spray even while I am not playing,' Labdhyo confided in me as we stood watching others play. 'But I have a back pain occasionally.'

'Good for you,' I answered back, knowing fully well that this man would go for his match on Monday at IIT KGP.

I could see a blazing fire in him, a profound energy, mixed with determination. When he stood on the field, guarding the goal post, he would turn into a completely different person—a pearl in the shell of an oyster. The broken shell forgot all the pain as he jumped to catch the ball, defending his team. I have seen so many human beings in love, but I have never seen anyone like Labdhyo, who was in love with his passion. They say pain is just a mere breeze when you walk on the path of love. It was true for Labdhyo.

His every gesture, be it the stretching of his arms and legs, or the way he would hold the ball, seemed to create a melodious harmony, a music of passion which broke through the physical pain and manifested itself in the spark of the keeper's eyes, and the blush of his smile. For everyone who is dedicated to his or her passion, watching him play is a treat!

'Ruud Shock has a very weak defence,' Labdhyo explained as I dropped by at his lab on Monday morning to enquire after his health.

'Labdhyo, I understand you are extremely passionate about the game, but . . .'

'But what, Aparajita?' This sudden use of my full name was a clear indication that he was extremely annoyed. I restrained from expressing any further anxieties.

'Umm . . . no . . . just wondering about today's defence!'

'Oh ho, we have Samit at left back and Joy at right back. Samit was in a different team in the FIIOB tourney, as you know,' Labdhyo's tone lightened. I dared not to bug him with any more questions.

'Here,' I placed the spray on his table. 'You might need it.'

'Thanks aJd', he smiled. 'No wonder the team calls you Chelsea's Eva.'

I nodded and left, worries creating a cacophony in my heart. They were beating drums of anxiety and the boisterous music of tension which consumed my enthusiasm for the upcoming tournaments.

In the days that followed, I had stopped bringing up the topic of his health altogether. I watched him play for his department where he captained the team, taking them to the final round. I didn't know what silenced me—the spectacle of his game or the zeal that overtook the pain and brought him victories. Perhaps both. The ninety-minute-long final match ended with extra time, which was followed by a penalty shoot-out.

'You guys don't have an extra goalie for a penalty shoot-out?' I almost broke down in tears as I saw Labdhyo preparing himself.

'None,' Nil confirmed.

The X-ray report, the doctor's words, and the heaps of painkillers I had seen lying on the table of his lab seemed to entangle me. His best friends, Nil and others, were aware of his health condition but nobody had the courage to approach him. They could not do without him. Even though I would speak little with them I sensed we were all on the same boat, vacillating between Labdhyo's health and supporting Labdhyo's team.

There were very few like him who were professional players when they were young but had not taken up the game as a career, celebrating the wall that separates passion from work; following the love of passion, and deliberately abstaining from the love of money. The Chemical Engineering Department of IIT KGP could boast of only one such player.

I wanted them to win. It was not the cup, rather the success of defending his team that made Labdhyo happy, that gave him the strength to fight against all odds, be it a shin injury or a massive back pain caused due to the slipped disc. Much to our dismay, his body betrayed him this time, landing them on the runner's up stage. He was proud of his team and he appreciated the way everyone played.

'I should have practised the penalty thing,' he sighed.

'How long, Labdhyo?' I could not control myself. 'How long are you going to put up with this and say you are "fine"? Am I that dumb that I can't understand the pain you are enduring?'

'Just the inter-hostel tournaments,' he assured me.

I knew it was coming. Being a struggling writer myself, I knew what it takes to be passionate about something. The defeats were not pulling him down; he cared little about them. The victories pushed him to soak up the pain. Painkillers allay the physical pain and a victory intensifies the drive to carry on. Even at twenty-eight, he would not retire. Even at twenty-eight, with a fragile body, he would lead his team towards victory. His eyes spoke of his love for the game. The love refuelled the waning energy. He exerted himself more by practising for penalty shoot-outs as the inter-hostel tournament approached. Nehru Hall was filled with just two words, 'Captain Labdhyo!' Even my friends from Sarojini Naidu Women's hostel came to cheer for Nehru.

Batman has been my most favourite hero since my childhood. Why? Because he is a hero without any magical power. He is driven by passion and intellect. I have always admired him, respected him. One might not be lucky enough to be born as a Kryptonian or as an Amazonian princess but dedication, hard work and endurance can make a Batman out of anyone. I was seeing one in front of me.

The inter-hostel tournament was the last of the football tournaments for the winter. Ignoring the setbacks, Labdhyo struggled on. His swollen right leg spoke of the pain he was enduring. I looked at him with awe as he brought victories to his hostel, round after round. Throughout these months, I saw a broken warrior fighting with the same spirit I had first seen him display. It reminded me of a few lines from the acclaimed Bengali writer, Saratchandra Chattyopadhyay's novel, *Pather Dabi*. Apurba, one of the main protagonists had thought in admiration, about the freedom fighter, Sabyasachi : *'It is perhaps you only who can take the onus upon your shoulders. That is why perhaps God has endowed upon you all the responsibilities and burden of this world.'* I felt the same about Labdhyo.

The final round of the inter-hostel football tournament was an engaging match between Nehru and R.K. Hall. Both the teams were in no position to give up. With their Messis and Cr7s they attacked but that day celebrated the existence of only one Neuer, whose struggle gifted this team with some stunning saves. Our Neuer, Labdhyo, stood proudly on the ground as his worthy striker, Rupak, managed to score a goal for his team around the seventieth minute. The opponents got into a complete attacking mode after that but Labdhyo had planned his defence well as a captain. He fiercely guarded his post and did not let a single shot enter the net. Finally, after the ninetieth minute, the stadium broke out in huge applause.

'Captain Labdhyo!' was the name that everyone voiced out.

His smile was brighter than his fluorescent jersey. Surrounded by his team mates and friends, he had defeated pain to have the last laugh. It was his day. He, the captain, had managed to give his team the victory they deserved.

I could not help myself from running up to him and giving him a hug.

'You did it, Labdhyo,' I said with tears in my eyes.

He smiled. 'Thank you.'

'You will have to help us win in the summer tournament of the FIIOB,' Rweeto smiled from behind.

'That is a completely different event!' Labdhyo exclaimed. 'How are you sure we will be in the same team?'

'We will buy you back no matter what!' Rweeto said with alacrity. 'This time, we will name our team, Ruud Re-awakening'.

'When did this brat come, aJd?' Labdhyo teased.

'In the afternoon,' I replied. 'He didn't want to miss your game. People are talking about you in the FIIOB.'

Labdhyo, like always, ignored the praise. Instead, taking his phone from me, he dialled a number.

'Hello, this is Labdhyo Mukherjee,' he said. 'I have been diagnosed with several injuries on my leg and a slipped disc, a few months back. I would like to make an appointment with the physiotherapist.'

And I saw the real Batman in front of me!

# A Daughter's First Flight

VIJAY KUMAR

If you are at an airport and see a passenger fumbling with either multiple children or many bags, or both—don't smirk and be sarcastic. Take it from me. That passenger could wind up in the seat next to you. The longer the flight, the greater the chance of this happening.

Here is my plight/story. I boarded a flight after spending four days in the biting cold of Delhi. I settled down in my seat, removed my shoes, and switched on my Kindle. My toes felt free and began to breathe again. Sighing deeply, I rested my head on the window pane and looked outside. The fog was descending on the city. The flight was full. It was time to get out of the winter and go home.

The pilot announced, 'We are waiting for one more passenger, then we will be on our way to Mumbai.' After his announcement ended, a lone figure appeared at the front end of the airplane. A harried girl with a small suitcase and two bags hanging from either side of her thin body. She clutched her mobile phone in her left hand. Her shawl kept slipping off her shoulder. She walked in, completely unaware of 120 impatient pairs of eyes staring at her.

'God is my witness,' I muttered. Huh! Lo and behold, the steward guided her to the empty seat, next to me! The passengers on the aisle and window seat always silently wish that the middle seat remains unoccupied so that it can be used as a side table to dump books, phones, and so on. But we were not so lucky.

She took forever to settle down in her seat. She put her carry-on and a shopping bag on her lap and looked for the seatbelt. I was getting annoyed as she occupied all the space and her stuff spilled over to my side. *Her last-minute shopping must have delayed her,* I thought.

'You are sitting on your seatbelt,' I said.

'I am sorry.' She got up holding all her stuff in both her hands.

I retrieved her seatbelt. She fumbled with the belt but couldn't get it right.

She was flying for the first time!

I fastened her seatbelt and noticed she clutched an additional boarding pass in hand.

'Where are you going?' I asked.

'Trichy . . . Tiruchirappalli,' she said, looking at me. Her narrow eyes behind her glasses were moist and red.

'What time is that flight?'

She looked at her boarding pass, '5.35 in the morning . . . Will there be a place at the Mumbai airport to charge my mobile phone?'

'Yes, of course. Don't worry, you have six hours to kill, enough time to charge your mobile phone,' I smiled. She could have taken a direct flight from Delhi to Trichy. She could have easily avoided spending six sleepless hours at the Mumbai airport. She was really clueless.

'Thank you.' She didn't catch the sarcasm in my voice. I ended the conversation and returned to my reading.

Soon I could hear sobs. She had covered her face with her hands and her body was shaking. She was crying.

'What is wrong?' I asked.

'Emergency . . . my father's in the hospital . . . very critical.' She removed her hands and looked at me with teary eyes.

'Oh dear . . . !' Suddenly, the fumbling and clumsy young woman disappeared and a little, sad and vulnerable girl tugged at me, a complete stranger. Such was her helplessness.

'I am so, so sorry. This is really sad but don't worry. He will be all right.' I let her cry. Her sadness and fear were personal.

While she cried, I looked at the tiny lights on the ground outside the window. We were gaining altitude as the aircraft made a turn and found its course.

Sadness turns strangers into friends. For the next hour she told me her story. Her name was Lisa and she lived in Tiruchirappalli with her older sister, mother and father. Her family had a history of lung disease. In her words 'Chronic Obstructive Pulmonary Disease'. She was a nurse and worked in one of the hospitals in Delhi. She had been looking forward to her first break to visit her family during the Easter holidays. She had bought a new shirt for her father last Sunday.

Lisa was the baby of the family and her father missed her a lot. He would call her up several times a day. Her father would have his lunch and call her to check if she had had hers. He would do the same after tea and dinner as well. I noticed a sad smile on her face when she talked about her father.

'This afternoon, I received a call on my mobile phone and saw "Daddy calling . . ." on the screen. I took the call and said, "Daddy, I had lunch."' Lisa recalled. But the voice was her neighbour's. And her father was not well. He was waiting for the ambulance to take him to the hospital. Lisa narrated the sequence of the day's events, 'My mother had gone to the market and my father was alone in the house.' She cried again. I gently touched the back of her hand with my fingertips.

'Why didn't you consider working in your hometown?' I asked.

'Hospitals in my town don't pay well. I came to Delhi six months ago to earn money so that I could pay for my father's treatment.'

I noticed that she kept taking her mobile phone out of her purse to check if there were any messages from home. She didn't know that mobile phones do not work at 35,000 feet above the ground. I didn't feel like telling her this fact. Facts sometimes damage hope.

The airhostess came by with the food trolley and parked it next to our seat. Lisa declined the supper, but I was hungry. I ate quickly and asked the airhostess for some hot water in my cup. I added sugar and slipped a tea bag in it. I gently forced Lisa to have the tea.

She held the cup in both her hands and looked at me, 'Are you a Father?' She wanted to know if I was Catholic like her and if I was a priest.

I said I was not, but taking the exhortation from 1 Peter, I said, 'You could say I am a pastor.' It was a perfect after-dinner conversation. The passenger in front of me had reclined his seat and almost put his head on my lap. The cabin lights were turned off.

The plane began descent to Mumbai. I love to take a night flight to Mumbai. From above, the city looks like a gorgeously lit-up planet. The plane landed, taxied and parked.

I grabbed her suitcase while she carried the shopping bag and other stuff. I had my bag checked in, so we waited for it. When you are not in a hurry, your bag will arrive in the first lot. My bag was the first to come. I snatched it off the carousel and looked for Lisa.

She was standing near a pillar amidst her bags, talking on the phone and crying. She had cupped her mouth. This cry was different. Instantly, I knew. I stood next to her watching her cry. She looked at me and shook her head. Every relationship, whether it's eleven minutes long or seven years old, creates its own language with words, looks, gestures and half-finished sentences.

'Lisa, I am so sorry. It's really very tragic,' I said. I offered to take her home and bring her back on time to catch her flight. She said she was fine and would wait at the airport. I looked for the airline staff to check if there were any flights earlier that she could take. There were none. I talked with two women staff members and shared Lisa's situation. They offered to take her to the departure lounge through a side door meant only for the employees.

I went back to Lisa and gave my phone number just in case she needed any help. I asked if I could pray for her. She nodded her head out of politeness. I prayed and when I opened my eyes I saw two women staff members standing with us with their eyes closed.

They escorted Lisa to the door. As she walked away, I noticed her shopping bag. It was a well-known men's clothing brand. Her father needed a new shirt. People were coming to see him.

# And Then the Planes Came

SANGHAMITRA BOSE

*'What are you doing outside? Why is your hand stretched out?'*

*'I am waiting for the bombs to fall.'*

*'Really! Come back in at once.'*

*I take one last look at the starlit sky, and follow Ma dutifully into the underground bunker. My dream of seeing bombs falling out of the sky like pretty raindrops, remains unfulfilled. Overhead, one can hear a high-pitched whine. The planes are coming. Ma hurries and quickly pushes me down into the bunker.*

The year was 1971. We lived in Ambala, a town on the Punjab–Haryana border. I had just turned three. My dad was an officer in the Indian Army and our home was a whitewashed army bungalow, situated alongside several others, in a quiet lane in the Ambala Cantonment. A front garden with a large jamun tree dominating the grassy patch and a backyard with a chicken coop was my world then. I spent my days on the makeshift wooden swing tied to the

jamun tree, or feeding the little chicks in the coop. My
mother tells me that I would sometimes wander out of the
backyard and into the mustard fields beyond, causing much
worry; I don't have any recollection of doing so. I do recall
my third birthday though. My mother had made a cake in the
shape of a doll and we had a small party with my friends from
the neighbourhood, under the jamun tree. The memory is
one of peace and tranquillity.

All that changed in December. In retaliation for what
they called 'unnecessary interference in our national matters',
Pakistan launched air strikes against India. Our prime minister
declared war and a massive operation was launched. Tremors
were felt nationwide, and Ambala was in the middle of it all.
It was close to the army's Western Command centre, and
chosen by the Pakistanis as a strategic target for air strikes;
overnight, the sleepy town became a mystified participant in
this juggernaut called war.

*Last night, Baba went away. Ma did not know that I was awake,*
*my eyes open as I lay in the baby cot. I saw him wear his uniform and*
*his shoes. He even stepped up to my cot and looked at me. I closed my*
*eyes and pretended to sleep. Then he went away. Ma told us the next*
*morning that Baba had gone to war. Didi and Dada asked her a lot*
*of questions. They were excited but Ma looked worried—like when*
*Dada does not come home on time. I wondered, why? Baba will fight*
*and win. Good people always do, like Hansel and Gretel burning the*
*bad witch and living happily ever after with their dad.*

The next morning the Cantonment was a bed of frenetic
activity. Trenches were being dug up in the lane in front
of our house, and sandbags and barbed wire was being set
in preparation for a sentry post. A team from our station
workshop arrived home to build an underground bunker in
the backyard. All the houses were to have bunkers, and we

were to immediately retreat to these when the air attack siren went on.

*The uncles from Baba's office came with big spades and other paraphernalia. They picked up our chicken coops and lined them along the backyard wall. The chicks were cheeping loudly, so I gave them some corn. Then I stood there and watched the uncles dig. Ma had told me not to disturb them. Soon they had dug a big hole in the ground. Ma told us that they were making a bunker for us to live in. Right now it looked like a big chicken coop. Then Ma called me in for lunch and a nap. When I went out in the evening, the hole was gone! There was grass there instead. I asked Didi where the hole was, and she laughed. Then she took my hand and led me to the grass. It seemed to be covered by a tent-like cloth. Didi flipped up the edge of the cloth. Ooh, there were secret steps going down! We climbed down and saw a big room. Ma and Sukhbir bhaiya followed us. They were carrying mattresses, pillows, blankets and a lantern, even!*

*'Ma, are we going to live here?'*

*'Maybe.'*

That night, as the air siren went off at 9 p.m., Ambala plunged into darkness. In accordance with strict wartime regulations, all lights were put out so that the raiding bombers would not be able to sight their targets—presumably the army headquarters and the ammunition depots. We got up immediately after we finished our dinner and made our way to the underground bunker. We kids were quite excited as was the dog. She could smell adventure a mile away. Settling in with biscuits and a big flask of tea, the dog sprawling across our tummies, I almost felt grown-up. For my pre-teen siblings, growing up on a fare of commando comics and *Biggles*, this was probably a dream come true. The excitement, tinged with apprehension, was palpable in the tiny room.

Meanwhile, the planes kept coming. We would hear a distinct whirr as the bombers flew in. This would be followed by distant sounds of explosions as their bombs found hapless targets on the ground.

*I awoke suddenly, not knowing where I was. In the feeble moonlight shining through the entrance of the bunker, I could see sleeping bodies all around me. In fact, there was one on top of me, letting out little canine snores. Pushing the dog away, I got up and stumbled over the others to reach the steps leading to the top. I slowly climbed these and stepped out into the moonlit night. There were no lights anywhere, except in the sky where a thousand stars twinkled. A few red dots could be seen in the dark horizon. They were moving steadily, coming closer. Maybe they were coming to drop bombs. In eager anticipation I stretched out my arms, wishing them to fall out of the sky and into my tiny, waiting hands.*

*'What are you doing here?'*

*Seeing Ma at the bunker steps, I told her without turning, 'I am waiting for the bombs to fall.'*

*Ma seemed to stand still; then she shook herself, ran out and dragged me into the bunker. 'Get inside at once,' she said. I could not help but sense an underlying tone in her voice, one that I had never heard before. Was it fear? Like what I felt when my brother told me ghost stories in secret? Anyway, I dutifully followed her into the bunker, the dog jumping up to lick my hand in a happy welcome.*

The morning after would bring news of bomb hits in the town. The air strikes were ceaseless and as the evening approached, a strange kind of tension would build up within our small family. We would sit around the big radio in the living room and hear nightly updates on the war. My mother heard this with particular concentration, her brow furrowed, her hands furiously working on her knitting. There were cheers when we took new ground and silence when we lost. More troops were called up as the Indian Army mounted its offensive.

*Today, Sukhbir bhaiya did not come home. I waited and waited, sitting on my swing. Maybe he was angry because I laughed at him yesterday.*

*'Bhaiya, why are you knitting?'*

*'Baby, I am knitting a sweater; for the soldiers who are fighting the war.'*

*'Silly Bhaiya! Only Ma and aunties knit. Men don't knit. They fight, didn't you know that?' I giggled.*

*Bhaiya smiled but he looked sad.*

*'Ma, why has Bhaiya not come today?'*

*'He has been called to fight the war, with Baba and the other uncles.'*

*'See, I was right! I told him yesterday that men fight, they don't knit. Ma, when will he return?'*

Sukhbir was our batman, my dad's man Friday and a willing partner in my three-year-old exploits. He would pluck jamuns for me, sit cross-legged so that I could line up my dolls on his lap, and then sing lullabies. He would push my swing so high that I could almost touch the leaves of the jamun tree. So his departure made a big difference to my small universe. I had no one to play with anymore. My mother had no time for me as she busied herself with the other army wives in a massive knitting operation. In a race against time, the ladies knitted a large number of sweaters, caps and mufflers for our soldiers battling the bitter north Indian winter.

With the schools shut for the winter holidays, the children in the lane had all the time to play and their games took on a distinct war flavour. Red Indians, commandos and the expected India vs Pakistan war games were replayed with equivalent passion on the grassy knoll at the end of the lane. I was not allowed to go out those days, but standing at the gate would give me a bird's-eye view to all that went on.

*I press my nose to the cold bars of the gate and peep to the right. I can see the jeep and the children standing around it. Didi's red ribbons are visible from afar. An uncle in uniform, pretty much like Baba's, stands talking to them. They are pointing here and there. I wish I was allowed to go out and join them. The group now walks closer—up to our front gate.*

*'There, there,' says Dada urgently, 'we were playing there, and the beggar walked up to us with our ball. "Why are you bachchas inside that trench?" he asked. "What is this for anyway? Is it a drain?"'*

*'And what did you boys tell him?' the uncle asks, sounding angry.*

*'We said that it was a trench for our soldiers to protect us from the Pakistanis,' Dada's friend pipes in. I can see Dada giving him a fierce stare, almost willing him to be quiet.*

*'Well, if you see him again, please tell your mother and ask her to call me at the station headquarters,' the uncle says, his tone gentler now.*

The espionage scare was one that I recall clearly. Suddenly, we had begun to see many beggars in the lane. Dirty, raggedy chaps who sat in the shade of the bungalow walls; in stark contrast to the whitewashed orderliness of the Army Cantonment. One of them had spoken to the children, asking them about the trenches. Then, the officer came one day and questioned the children. It turned out that the beggars may have been Pakistani spies, trying to uncover important security information. This was a strategy adopted at both ends, the Indian Army having done similar cloak-and-dagger stuff in erstwhile East Pakistan, now Bangladesh, prior to the war. In fact when I grew older, I was told that one of my father's colleagues—a tall, smart gentleman—worked as a cobbler for many months in Dacca, collecting crucial espionage information. In any case, it was additional fodder for the imaginative minds of the children.

And then the war ended. With the declaration of a ceasefire, the warfare came to a sudden stop. Troops and officers started returning home. We would see the olive green jeeps, rolling down our lane, dropping off familiar faces at each gate. My Dad was one of these. My mother lay down her knitting and started smiling again, my siblings got ready to go to school once more, and Ambala got its lights back.

*Today Sukhbir bhaiya came back. He picked me up and swung me high. He even got some barfi for me. I am really happy to see him back. He has promised to play with me and the dolls later on, after he finishes polishing Baba's shoes. I can't wait!*

My tiny existence was back to its mundane routine. With the bunker bricked up, we could move the chicken coops back to where they belonged and I could go out for a walk in the lane with my ayah once more. However, something had changed within us. Our family became more closely knit—the experience of war seeming to have been a splash of cold water on our hitherto idyllic existence. I think my parents and siblings would re-assess their life's priorities, whilst I was just happy about Sukhbir bhaiya coming back.

As an adult, I have had occasion to go back to Ambala and have re-visited the lane of my childhood, a couple of times. The house still stands, worse for wear after forty years. The garden and the jamun tree seem smaller, seen through adult eyes—the lane narrower and unpaved. The little grassy knoll at the end of the lane still remains and I see children playing on it, as I used to, many years ago. The serene surroundings belie the tension and excitement that had swept us all up, many years ago. It is almost as if the war never happened.

I still remain wary of planes.

# Breaking the Impasse

SHAILY BHARGAVA

There was a sudden zephyr of bittersweet memories zipping me in a nostalgic coma as I boarded the flight. Air travel had not seemed so tough until today. Two members of the gentle cabin crew somehow led me to my aisle seat. There was turbulence, not in the flight but in my head—mental and emotional. I could only half concentrate on the inside of the flight; a part of me was still stuck in the corridors of the hospital. The white lights over my head were stupefying my brain, confusing the flight and hospital.

'Are you okay?' asked the concerned middle-aged gentleman in the seat next to mine.

'Hmmm.'

'Indian?'

'Hmmm.'

'I am also going to Kolkata. I had been working in Sydney for the last two years but miss Kolkata terribly, especially during the Durga puja. Kolkata is beautiful during . . .'

'Shut up,' I snarled and closed my eyes to cut off the unnecessary torture. I had my inhibitions and apprehensions about his city.

~

A week ago . . .

I had been on a different phase in the office when my narcissistic manager, the fat David Pope, a stud among the mules, announced, 'You are promoted, Ady!'

Those words were music to my ears and my heart blared out Honey Singh's loud party song when suddenly, David continued, 'So there's an important conference scheduled next week, attended by top corporate and media executives of South Asia. Ady, you will be representing our company there. Oh, and it's in Kolkata, India.'

The second last word hit me like a bullet and I sank into a chair, pale and dull.

*Kolkata, Kolkata!* I said in my head and was insane enough to finally declare, 'No, David, I can't go!'

'Well, then I am afraid the management might reconsider your promotion.'

'What? You got to be kidding me, David . . .' I said in mock surprise and he shrugged boorishly, 'My way or go away.'

Hence I, Aditi Sharma, aka Ady, would visit Kolkata again!

~

'Ma'am, anything for you?' blinked the pretty airhostess, breaking my reverie.

'O yes, can you please make me disappear into thin air?'

'Ma'am, I'm afraid that is not an option,' she chuckled and served me a glass of wine.

I sipped some wine in the twenty-hour-long Sydney–Kolkata flight and eventually passed out, switching back to that time when . . .

Kolkata, 1991. . .

Year after year, lots of children visit the City of Joy attracted by the Howrah Bridge, Victoria Memorial and rosogulla.

Well, twenty years ago, I was one of them. However, I was not there for the food or monuments. I visited the city to get a healthy heart in the city's finest heart institute.

It was the first time I had missed my school for treatment of a disease I had no knowledge of. I had informed my friends innocently that a small bug had gotten into my heart and that it would be fixed by doctors in no time.

I was a cute, pampered, courteous six-year-old chatterbox. A week into the treatment, I became friends with Divya, the patient on the next bed. We played Ludo and sometimes read story books together. I wandered around the children's ward or peeked into the nurse station and the doctors smiled when nurses sent me back to bed.

There were just two things abnormal about me. Firstly, I had jet engines fixed in my legs (according to my mother, as I rarely ever sat in one place for long) and had a curious mind that threw up uncountable questions. Secondly, I had been diagnosed with chronic heart disease, a ventricular septal defect, and pulmonary arterial hypertension at the time of birth. I had been restricted from doing any tiresome activity, no running, less walking and easy living for the sake of living longer. Like other children, I attended school. But my school time did not include the sports period and the morning assembly. My friends played in the school grounds and parks while I sat in a corner. They participated in group activities like the school choir or physical games while I cheered for them from the sidelines. In short, I had the dos and don'ts list imprinted in my head from the day I was born. If I dared to enter the 'DON'T', I faced high blood pressure, a little nose or mouth bleed and a few injections with a warning to take a sincere week-long rest. After kindergarten, I started to rebel against the monotonous medical routine.

*Wasn't it a lot to expect from a six-year-old to acclimatize herself to a boring, restricted life?*

I would not have any of it!

The Kolkata hospital had famous, successful doctors and surgeries to their credit. I was overjoyed! Finally, the day had come. I was pushed towards the operation theatre. My parents cheered for good luck by animatedly raising their thumbs up in the air.

'Nervous, Ady?' whispered the doctor.

'So after today, I can swim, sing in choirs, and participate in badminton matches?'

'Yes, definitely.'

'Then just go for it,' I murmured.

*Four hours later in the cardiac care unit . . .*

My eyes felt heavy and the white light above my head almost seemed to blind me. It took a great amount of strength to open my mouth or flutter the eyelids, as if I was waking up after ages. I could not feel the left side of my body.

I try to slowly raise my arms. I manage with some effort. Both right and left. I sigh with relief. Now legs . . . left side of the body still felt numb. The toes on my right leg moved, and now, left . . . left . . . left leg did not respond! I gasped and a knife of fear pierced deep in my heart with thin films of tears clouding my eyes. I tried once, twice, and then I screamed as loud as my fragile body could in the quiet CCU.

I cried, rather ordered, incessantly, 'Call my mommy and daddy!'

'What she says is not possible, Mr Sharma. We operated on her heart not legs; she is just in post-surgery trauma. She'll be fine. We are sorry but the surgery was not successful. We were hopeful for a complete recovery but unfortunately, it didn't go as we thought it would. Her problems stay the same,' whispered the doctor to my disappointed parents.

'Hey, we would be going home soon, Ady!' my father said, trying to sound cheerful, entwining his big fingers in mine.

'I can't feel my left leg,' I cried with the same complaint for hours.

Ultimately, the doctors came down to check.

Minutes turned into hours as I cried insistently and the doctors kept running tests and scans the whole day. And then something utterly devastating happened that we never thought or imagined.

'Fibrosis. Aditi has got fibrosis due to which the sensation of her left leg has completely gone.'

'But how . . . umm, her legs were perfectly fine before the surgery.'

'Umm, the hospital is sorry. We can talk about it, sir.'

'How did this happen to my daughter?' cried my father in disbelief.

'Medical negligence . . . I was late so to save time a junior nurse . . . the injection . . . she pricked it into a wrong vein. You see, we have fired her,' offered the doctor nervously, yet confidently, still trying to save his name and the hospital's reputation.

Conveniently termed as 'medical negligence' that shockingly took away everything from the six-year-old Ady, who only some time back was hopeful of walking away hale and hearty; the little girl who had played with the nurses was now a handicapped girl learning how to walk with crutches! Pain, fear and shock hit my little mind.

I became hostile, stubborn and cranky. I hated everybody, the nurses, doctors, even my grandparents who called persistently every day to hear my voice. Divya went home, another crop of patients who took her place also went back cured but I stayed on for days, weeks and months. The five-by-three-feet window next to my bed secretly showed me Kolkata—the sound of its traffic and people. I remember never having drawn the curtains the time I was there. Everybody had a routine around me. The hospital staff, the visitors, my parents. I also started developing one. Every night, I closed my eyes softly after taking medicines and then tenderly smiled and imagined a happier world where I ran, jumped, watched my favourite cartoons, enjoyed junk food and ice creams.

In my dream world I watched the sunrise while taking a boat ride on the Hooghly river under the Howrah bridge. Early morning, I heard the birds chirping and imagined my friends waiting for me back in school. Yes, some days, it did dawn on me that there was nothing, absolutely nothing and nobody. Although the days were new, for me it was all dark, pitch-dark, with the same medicines, same nurses in the same hospital room with the same dead leg that felt nothing. The window was my only source of merriment. I couldn't move and I couldn't see out from it but I had a routine, my routine in that Kolkata hospital room that had been a jail for three long months. I was a lab rat on whom they tried their tricks and experiments. I was drained of my cute smiles, laughter, courage and spontaneity. I pledged never to visit the city again, innocently telling my parents, 'I have had enough of Kolkata.'

Since then, I grew up with a thought: Kolkata took away everything.

Kolkata now scared the hell out of me!

~

The dark days of my dead leg were not over yet when we reached Delhi for my leg surgery. The chances for recovery were rare but we decided to give it a shot. At the same time, my uncle informed my father about a Sardarji, an acupuncturist in Faridabad who had some miraculous cases to his credit.

Only five hours were left for the hospital appointment when the idea of consulting Sardarji came up, leaving us in two minds. To our rescue came Mr Sethi, my uncle's NRI friend settled in Australia whose son had met with an accident that had left his lower body with severe fibrosis. He was walking after rigorous treatment with Sardarji.

Allopathy and acupressure—both gave no surety. The doctor's appointment was fixed after relentless requests and if we missed this one, it would take six more months to get another. The Sardarji was available all the time, without any appointment.

A cloud of uncertainty and bewilderment surrounded us.

Around noon, I once again settled in the car for another hospital, another surgery, and another mystery. We drove through the traffic with hope and fear. The car stopped at a traffic signal. There were two roads leading from there. Straight ahead, the hospital was 12 kms away, and a turn to the right would take us to Sardarji's home.

And, we turned right!

No reason, no confusion but once again with a ray of hope and to find the lost sparkle in my laughter, my parents turned the car.

~

Harvinder Sodhi glanced around the vanilla cream walls
of a large hall that led to a compact room which he had
called his clinic for the past thirty-seven years. He noticed
us entering his premise, sighed and folded his *Dainik Jagaran*
as he rose from the sofa. I was in my father's lap, with a
serious and cranky face. He walked towards us in brown
khaki pants and a white shirt, flashing a bright affectionate
smile for closer introspection.

That I didn't want to have anything to do with this man
was clear from my face.

He opened and closed my right palm in a flash. I reopened
it and there was a Cadburys Éclair! Everybody smiled and
somehow a weak smile crossed my face for a second.

That very day, he started the rigorous treatment of hard
and painful massages—massages that brought uncountable
tears and shrieks from me! I thought that the electric
current treatment by the Kolkata hospital was better than
Sardarji's way.

Each day I cried, begged my parents not to take me to
Faridabad, but they did. They were more helpless than me.
They felt my pain, and cried when I screamed in pain but they
trusted Mr Sodhi. They were putting their trust in the power
of faith.

A month passed by in Delhi. Then four months breezed
past, away from school, away from my friends. I had almost
forgotten my life before Kolkata but I yearned for it. Every
time I looked at the sixty-five-year-old Sardarji, he simply
smiled. I verbally abused him with '*chodo budhu*, idiot, stupid',
even frightened him, 'the police will take you' and eventually
begged in the three-hour-long massage sessions for my legs
but he stayed unperturbed, smiling. I hated that smile—the
very same smile, I witnessed on day one, no change, same

confident eyes and words, 'She will walk soon and even run. Fibrosis is nothing; your daughter has a long way to go, Sharma sahib.'

~

I felt a vibrant buzz inside my trousers. The mobile alarm had gone off, bringing me back from my little trip to 1991. I slowly blinked my eyes trying to recollect where I was. I stretched my arms and pulled myself up on the seat when my eyes met with my co-passenger.

He smiled. I ignored him.

The lights were still off. I had the middle seat. The right side passenger was in deep sleep. The guy on the left was busy watching a movie. There was not a single drop of wine left either in the glass or in my body. I was hungry as hell. Suddenly, the Bong passed a packet of cookies to me. I looked at the packet and then looked back at him. He was glued to the movie. I waited for some twenty-odd seconds but he continued to stare at the screen. Was he rude or was I discourteous?

The movie finished and so did the small cookie packet. I picked two more from the airhostess's tray later.

'Thanks,' I murmured looking at him.

'It's okay, beta.'

Post-1991, I preferred to talk less to strangers, especially Bengalis.

'You feel okay now?' the man enquired, with concern.

'Ummm . . . I'm good now.'

'You don't like the place you are visiting?' he asked but then immediately checked himself, 'You don't have to answer that, sorry.'

Well, for the sake of the cookies that he had shared, I softly replied, 'I hate Kolkata.'

Silence hung between us. I saw his forehead crease into deep lines, his caring big eyes behind the black, thick frames widening and his confident smile fading. He reminded me of somebody very familiar, very true, a selfless, kind man but very harsh and painful at the same time.

'Sardarji?' I mumbled under my breath, astonished.

Of course he wasn't Sardarji! He was a Bengali from Kolkata.

The man then introduced himself as Ashutosh Banerjee, and asked the reason for my hatred towards his city, a city that's called the 'City of Joy'!

Five more hours were left, so with a heavy heart I narrated my story, my journey to Kolkata.

Tears poured out as I narrated the story. But after it was over, I felt serene and drank some cold water to calm my disturbed nerves.

'Hmm . . . shall we open this packet of cookies too? I think you like them, huh?' Mr Banerjee tittered, changing the topic.

I gobbled down two more while he watched me.

'Oh, what happened to the Sardarji's treatment?'

I laughed and joyfully replied, 'He was right, I really went a long way from thereon, walking on my two legs!' I chuckled. 'Sixteen weeks of dedicated treatment and some ten buckets of tears made me stand and walk again without the crutches. He killed the fibrosis. Those confident eyes and smile won!'

I opened another packet and to my disappointment, the first cookie had no choco-chip on it. I brooded.

'It happens sometimes—the packet you so cheerfully tore has this cookie with no choco-chip. Now what will you do? Throw the packet and buy a new one or will you go ahead hoping this was a miss but the next cookie might have enough chips on it? Your thoughts are so vivid, perplexed and tangled around the contours of your last experience of the hospital's five-by-three-feet glass window that remotely showcased Kolkata to your six-year-old mind. What's gone is gone. Mr Sodhi killed the fibrosis in you but sadly, you didn't kill the scepticism and fear within you. Realize Sardarji's words in every sense—you have a long way to go, overcome your bias of Kolkata. You are young and intelligent. I believe you should not get stuck in the corridors of old times and keep your mind open for new images and memories.' Mr Banerjee smiled as he gave his smart yet modest piece of advice.

The plane landed at Netaji Subhash Chandra Bose International Airport with the first rays of the sun.

While waiting for the taxi, I reopened that cookie packet. To my surprise, leaving the first blank cookie, the entire batch had choco-chips sprinkled evenly!

'For how long will you hold resentment against something that had happened twenty years ago?' whispered my conscience.

I realized it was time to break the protracted impasse between the two of us—Kolkata and me. I rebooted my mind with the subtle early morning breeze, slightly serene in its zest, looping me in the fancy of fresh Kolkata. The soft sun rays had started to subsume the darkness. The slate of my mind and heart turned blank and a tender smile stretched over my face. I screamed in delight, permitting the contemporary Kolkata to greet me one more time, erasing the bitterness, rolling me crisply in its sweetness.

'*Kothai jaaben madam* . . . where do you want to go, madam?' asked a taxi driver.

'To the ghat for a morning boat ride on the Hooghly river,' I chirped.

# Clean Slate

SUKANYA M.

She writhed and winced and convulsed and seeing her do all these things left me transfixed. I would have continued to stare had my aunt not shut my eyes with her hand and almost dragged me out of the room. She put me to bed, placed a blanket over me, and whispered in my ears that my mom was going to be fine and walked out. In spite of her outward composure it was evident that the incident had shaken her too.

I tossed and turned as my fear escalated with every passing second till I finally gave in to sleep.

When I awoke, it took me a while to figure out that we were travelling in a car. I was seated on my aunt's lap. She told me that we were on our way to the hospital where my mom was admitted. Then she instructed me to go back to sleep, perhaps to silence any further questions, to which, I suspect, she herself had no answers.

After a while, I woke up and the smell typical of hospitals that my nostrils registered confirmed that we were there at last.

There was a deathly silence about the place interrupted only by the screeches of the wheels of the stretchers and the sounds made by those who walked or talked (rarely). The silence amplified the million horrifyingly torturous questions inside our heads.

For some time I followed my dad who was walking into counters and consulting rooms, paying bills for different laboratory tests and other such expenses. He wore a serious and worried expression, and was perspiring in an air-conditioned hall. Reason one, because my mom's health reports were showing dire results; the second reason was money. Detection and treatment of diseases cost money and there wasn't that much to spend for a lower middle class family like ours!

Beside me, my grandma had started chanting hymns—she felt praying could help my mom to overcome the adversity so I forwarded my own prayer: 'O God, please help my mom get better. And by better I mean out of the hospital and healthy enough to be doing all the things she was doing. Else you might lose some of the believers of your miracles. This is your test, God. Hope you fare well.'

I know challenging the ego works with humans but I didn't know how it was with God. I hoped that it would have the same effect. With these thoughts I ended the prayer feeling more hopeful. After all I had just done all that I could.

It seemed like we waited in those corridors for an eternity with no updates about what was happening inside.

Not until the needle on the hospital's clock swept a lazy 180 degree did something happen. But when it happened, it was all too quick. I could spot more familiar faces entering the hospital. And it was no coincidence. I was later informed that they had come there to give us both financial and moral support. For families like ours, the most important asset is people and their goodwill which translates into help at times of need.

Long spells of quiet followed. I whiled away the time by reading and memorizing signboards that was put up here and there on the hospital walls. I read them once, twice, thrice, and finally after I'd read them the fourth time, I knew I needed to find another way to pass my time.

Actually the habit of reading anything I see was drilled into me by my mom. She insisted that I read every signboard on the road wherever we travelled. It was her idea to help me read fast and learn pronunciation. It was a challenge I had liked when I was a kid. Such thoughts made me miss my mom, who now lay unconscious and alone in the sterilized room with masked people and beeping machines.

I had to think of some way to divert my mind. The only rescue was the coffee corner at the hospital. I nagged my grandma to take me there, cooking up a desire for coffee. Before I could finish sipping the steaming coffee, the walls of the hospital echoed with our ringing cell phone. We were asked to come to the ward immediately.

And what I saw there was a picture of hysteria. I spotted my uncle in a frenzy walking towards me; yes, a bigger part of my family was now there in the hospital premises.

I could not read a thing from his expression. That's the thing about adults, isn't it? Their faces never show how they feel inside! When he was close enough, and I confident enough that I was audible, I mouthed a single word, 'Mom?'

He responded in three words, 'She is dead.'

This time it was I who became blank, not just in my expression but in my mind as well.

The hospital sounds appeared to be muted to me. But for moments, I am not sure how long or short, the noise within shook me!

'She is DEAD!'

'My mom is DEAD.'

'MY MOM is DEAD.'

One big question buzzed in my mind, 'What is THAT supposed to mean?'

Honestly, I didn't know what I was supposed to feel. Till then I had seen death as a part of a movie or a story. And all of a sudden, something I'd thought was alien and abstract to me had already become my reality.

I saw a hospital staff member handing over my mom's jewellery to my dad and then my mom was packaged into the ice box, moved into an ambulance while we boarded our hired car back home.

Death, I believe, is not an experience for the dead but for the living. A crowd was already waiting at our home, family and friends at three in the morning! Sending off the dead to heaven is an elaborate process, ritual after ritual continued; and that I guess is so because it helps to register the fact that the dead is dead.

Tears, tears and tears everywhere, everyone was crying, was offering their condolences and consolation to people she was attached to, which obviously included me. Aunties and uncles whom I could not even recognize, whose names I didn't know, offered their sympathies to me. Personally, for me, it was a kind of humiliating experience to be at the receiving end of their sympathy. While I was struggling to figure out what all of this meant to me, people around me understood the situation in their own way. According to them, this was the most devastating and crippling event in my life, the dent this had created in my destiny was irrevocable, irreparable and I was eternally cursed with motherlessness.

Still I didn't cry. My eyes seemed as dry as a desert. The numbness hadn't worn off yet. I behaved like a video recorder. My eyes saw all it could, my ears heard all they had to, just that I did not and could not react to any of it.

Finally, the inevitable happened. She was taken to the graveyard. It was only then that I shed my first tears. My tears, my grief, was for a fellow human who had been, for most part of her four-decade long life, identified by her physical self, was to be erased out of existence. Except, of course, the countless memories of her that we would carry around all our lives.

After a week, the elders got into the 'life-must-go-on' mode and all of us made an effort to fall back into our routines.

It was another jolt of reality that our routine was no more the same; we had a missing link. I moved in with my maternal grandparents while my father moved in with his widowed sister who lived with one of her brother-in-laws and his family. This was the best set-up we could come up with then (strictly elders' decisions).

Did I feel sad? Actually, I was not supposed to and mostly I didn't, because my grandparents, my uncles, my aunts went out of their way to pamper me and guard me from the harsh realities of being motherless.

However, the realization of what her death signified came to me in doses.

One day, my uncle stayed back to help me with my school work and that particular assignment got me extra credits. I called him up and thanked him profusely. I had always earned accolades and appreciation for whatever I had done with my mom's help as well, yet not even once had I taken a moment to share a good word with her about it.

The penultimate episode that erased my numbness happened when one of her friends (yes, her friendships were alive even after she had left the world) stopped by to gift me a story book, *The Malgudi Days* by R.K. Narayan. I thanked her friend as much as I could for her affection. She tearfully returned my 'thanks', and said it was she who had to thank me for my sheer existence because I was a beautiful reminder of a beautiful person who had left the world. And how doing something for me, helped her miss my mom less. I stood there rooted, taking in all the emotions of loss, grief, friendship and love.

Surprisingly for someone like me who hated books, I finished the novel in the next two days. My new-born love for books was the best parting gift my mom had left for me.

Did I miss my mom? Did her absence choke me to tears? Actually, no. As a matter of fact I was only now noticing the presence my mom had had in my life! Till then whatever she did, I had taken for granted. It was her absence that spoke loudly of her presence to me.

I sank in my tears when it struck me that I had been so blind to all her love and care, that I had missed acknowledging the person who was deserving of many 'thanks' and much more, which I was conveying to others now.

I hated myself for the apathy I had shown my mom and the bitterness and the dislike I had displayed because I didn't like her going to work, leaving me be on my own. It seemed to me then that spending time with me was her last option. I began to realize with shame that she was busy building support for my future, on which I was to thrive from now on—both financially and morally.

Forgiving myself became even more difficult when I read an excerpt from her journal:

'. . . *such an angel she is, a lot of times I envy my mom who gets to take care of my daughter for most of the time. The only time I get with her is when she is almost asleep. Had it not been for the tablets that put me to sleep, I'm sure I could spend nights just looking at her . . . to hell with my work! It never leaves me with any time for her. How much I wish to just quit my job and be with her full time like she asks me to! But that is not a possibility if I want the best for her, and she deserves nothing less, this angel . . .'*

My guilt grew to such heights that I began to feel that it was because I was so undeserving of my mom that the gods had to call her back to heaven!

But I didn't have to live with the guilt for a long time. All I had to do to get out of the self-inflicted misery was flip through a few more pages of her journal and there it was, a note from her:

'. . . *after the brain surgery, they call it a miracle that I am able to function normally. I am even going to resume work in a few months. But if it is a miracle that all this is happening, I would attribute it to my little Anjali . . . She was my only inspiration to come back to life . . . it is a joke that it was I who brought her to life. This wonder girl whom I happened to mother is the only reason the gods had spared me. It was she who brought me my life for one other time . . .'*

It was a relief after I read it. Maybe she wrote it when she was too emotional, nevertheless, I was in a phase in which I understood that our feelings make most of what we perceive as reality.

The final incident that happened before I fully internalized and digested my mom's death occurred when I was taken to meet my father, after many months.

We first stopped at a bank where we had to sign some papers so that the money that was credited to us from the workplace of my mother would be used for my benefit.

The next stop was the house he lived in. It was news to
me that he had moved out of my aunt's. A not very young
lady opened the door. A lot of silence followed, in which the
lady went off to make tea and my father and I settled in on the
cushions. To break the silence, my dad spoke. He introduced
me to the woman there, my name, school, grade, and that I
was intelligent and all that blah. I put on a smile as the lady
nodded her head. To put things in context, he introduced the
woman to me—one single statement after which an awkward
silence followed.

'She is my wife,' he said.

I absorbed it. I nodded my head, I didn't quite know what
else or how else to respond. I could feel my legs go weak. I was
happy that I was already seated. Within me I could feel all the
emotions that humanity would have endured when Nicholas
Copernicus had first proved that the earth was indeed spherical
and not flat!

There is this noise that one hears when one's beliefs are
shattered, a noise that will want you to wish that you were
deaf lest you hear it. This was exactly what happened when I
heard him say that. Till then I had believed as a fact that only
one's mom could be one's dad's wife, but I was proven wrong,
partially wrong, if I may say so.

The atmosphere was fraught with emotions and anxiety.
The place felt strangely familiar, familiar because I could see
the things which I had grown up with—the sofa, the curtains,
the table etcetera, strange because I felt disowned even amidst
these familiar things!

I could not avoid looking at the woman for long and
from what I saw it seemed to me that she was not half bad
as Cinderella's stepmom. But that was not enough for me to
accept her as family.

'I am going back to Grandma's, right?' I wanted immediate confirmation. I could not stay there any longer.

My dad started to say something, but all that he ended up saying was, 'Yes.' What a relief!

'You should know it is not like what you think.'

I wanted to ask him what he thought I was thinking because I myself had difficulty placing my thoughts! People always assume what you are thinking or how you are feeling!

'It is an adult thing, I am sure you will understand me when you are older. I want you to understand that I had wished you a mother as much as I wished myself a wife . . .'

'O my God! Will you please cut the crap out?' I wanted to say.

'. . . life should go on, you see? The point is that I felt so lonely, vulnerable, and afraid to go through it alone, so I had to do this. So I had to do this . . .'

He was breaking down. There were tears in his eyes. I quickly said, 'Dad, it is your life. You need not explain anything to me. Let us save ourselves from this discussion, please.'

So that was the truth. He had succumbed to pity unlike me who found her great love, fortunately or unfortunately, after her demise.

My grandparents were obviously very disturbed by his re-marriage. I didn't allow myself to be bothered by it much, because like they say, it was out of my locus of control. So I just let it pass, and eventually, everybody else did the same.

And yes, life went on. But there was a huge difference now. I had figured out so many things through all this.

Of all those, the greatest discovery and learning was that, as they say, through the labour pain a woman goes through death and is born again as a mother. This time my mom went through death and didn't make her journey back. But the thing is, I was born again. As clean as a slate. But this time I was careful about what was going to be written into me as beliefs, facts and faiths. In ways that cannot be explained through human language, I am confident that her death taught me more than what a hundred lives would have. It is not to be understood that she thought of me as someone who would be unable to pick up life lessons like an average person. Her intention, if there was one, was to fast-track my learning.

'Godspeed' was her farewell wish to me for the journey called life!

# Divine Intervention

## MADHURIE PANDIT

The day of 1 September 2012 was truly special, not only because it was my birthday, but because I discovered what true, non-materialistic happiness means.

I had gone to a mall with my daughter. There was no plan as such. So we decided to check out last minute ticket availability for a movie. Sadly, none of the movie timings matched our schedule.

It was too early to have lunch so we decided go to the gaming zone. We went to the counter and bought a swipe card for playing games. My daughter took some time to decide the sequence in which she wanted to play games.

Suddenly, I noticed a small child pulling his father in all possible directions. From the appearance it looked as if the man had got his child to the mall only for a stroll. Needless to say, he could not afford gaming zone charges.

The child was keen on sitting on the merry-go-round in the gaming zone but his father said no and took him to watch the bumping cars instead. It was supposed to be the only visual treat for that child.

Though my daughter and I were busy playing games, my thoughts and eyes were keenly following that little child. Was it his father's fault that he could not play games there? Was it their financial position?

Destiny? Karma? There was a tsunami of thoughts in my mind . . .

It was making me sad, very sad . . .

After a while I gathered my courage and went to his father. I asked him, 'Would your son like to enjoy a ride on the merry-go-round?'

His father refused shyly.

I was disappointed but I tried to persuade him. I lied to him. I said, *'Mere pass bonus points hai, jo main use nahi karne wali. Aap* please *apne bete ko* merry-go-round *main baithne dijiye na.'* I told him about some bonus points I had on my card and that they could be used for a ride for the child. This trick worked! He gladly agreed.

Pointing to the merry-go-round, I asked his son, *'Aap us main baithenge?'* (Would you like to sit on it?) Suddenly, there was a smile on his face. He nodded his head with happiness. I swiped my game zone card and let him enjoy one round. My daughter and I stood watching this boy enjoy the ride. I saw him secretly looking at me with those beautiful eyes, which were filled with happiness. After one round was over, I asked him if he wanted to repeat. He nodded his head faster than the first time . . . So I swiped my card again for one more round.

His father gave me a look, which didn't need any words.

After that round, I let that boy enjoy one more ride on a different game. By then my daughter had decided which game she wanted to play, so we moved on.

Now my mind was calm and I was feeling better. The tsunami of thoughts ebbed. While we were busy playing, this boy and his father came to me to say thank you. His father's 'thank you' said a million words. That boy's face was brimming with happiness and contentment.

It was truly a Kodak moment, which I could not capture as I was busy seizing every bit of happiness and peace that I felt amidst the noisy surroundings.

Now when I think about it, everything seemed so pre-planned by the universe . . . Why did we decide to go to the mall? . . . Why had none of the movie timings matched our schedule? . . . Why we landed at the gaming zone . . . Perhaps that boy was destined to enjoy the game rides . . . And I was chosen by God to fulfil his wish!

I guess that's what we call 'divine intervention'.

The cost of that boy's happiness was Rs 120 but the satisfaction and peace that filled my heart was worth millions.

This episode made my birthday truly memorable. There couldn't have been a better way to celebrate a birthday, could there?

# Suicide (So Decide)

PRASANTHI POTHINA

We get to live life once, stop wasting it, by deciding to die because of silly mistakes!

As I sat on the lone rock, the waves looked very inviting. I had just one thought in mind—to jump into the water! Yes, I was actually considering ending my life and the thought of a watery death was welcome. I had tried the train tracks, but then had freaked out at the last moment.

Now I was testing the waters, literally, but an angel, and I would definitely call him one, shooed me away from the rock. He was a policeman on his daily rounds.

'Ma'am, you'd better get down from there, it's not that safe.' His suspicious eyes would not leave me unattended for a second. I was happy for his presence because I was chickening out on this plan too.

I got down from the rock and walked back to my car, the cool breeze kept playing with my hair, the salt spray hit my face. But there was more salt in the tears of frustration which were pouring down my face than the spray.

It was past 7 p.m. now. Vinay would be home and reading my ill-fated letter, which I had written this morning. He must be calling me on my cell. I had switched it off.

I think Ram must have been trying my number too. God, why was I thinking of that two-timing idiot! I could not believe I had led myself into this situation. It was horrible! No one could have saved me from the doom I faced. And I had no one to blame but myself.

I was happy to give Ram a piece of my mind at the airport. How stupid of me to have fallen for his false praise and sweet nothings! My arrival at the airport at exactly 4.30 in the evening had been a winning sign for him. Somehow, his very angelic and handsome face looked crude and ugly to me now. He had tried to embrace me; I shrank from his touch.

'What's the matter, darling, where is your luggage?'

I looked at him straight in the eye, 'Well, for your kind information, people do not travel with their extra-marital relations!' Saying this I'd slapped his face and turned and ran out of the airport. I don't know if he understood what I told him. I didn't even give him time to explain. In the morning he had been like a Greek god, an escape channel for me. Now, in the evening, his looks had faded.

Actually, this morning started on a very different note; the disturbance I was feeling now was non-existent. I had cooked lunch like an obedient wife, done my daily chores and said bye to my husband Vinay and closed the door.

At that time it was a final goodbye. I was happily married to him for five years. He was a regular guy who my parents had selected for me. As destiny would have it, we moved out of his parents' house after a month of our marriage. Vinay was calm, never demanding. If some day I did not feel like cooking, he would either do it himself or get food from outside. Whatever I asked him for he would buy, never complain, never even scolded me. But this was not enough for me. He was not passionate. I was a wild one and I missed the roughness of life.

Like a miracle, one day his cousin Ram, a software engineer, visited us. He had to stay with us for a job training process. It was a three-month call, but three minutes were enough to sweep me off my feet! My blouse necklines went lower and sarees became more transparent. I was least interested in cooking earlier but I suddenly developed a huge interest in making new dishes. I never bothered about the time Vinay returned home but was always anxious for Ram.

Imagine if someone softly called you beautiful in your ear and touched you without your husband's knowledge, a sudden kiss on your lips when you were cutting vegetables, a peck on the back, a hot embrace right behind your husband's back—it was like a challenge that always turned my cheeks red.

He had the nerve to say 'I love you!' in front of my husband.

It so happened that Vinay had got hot samosas on a Sunday evening. All three of us were watching a movie and suddenly I began hiccupping. Vinay got me water, sugar . . . what not, but the hiccups just wouldn't stop.

They tried to scare me by shouting at me but the hiccups would not subside. Suddenly Ram got up from the sofa, came right up to me and said, 'I love you, Sandhya.' That was it. Vinay looked wide-eyed; as for me, I nearly fainted.

Then he smiled, 'See your hiccups have vanished!' That was true, they sure did vanish, but my heart was racing fast.

Later, the next day, when Vinay left for office early, and we finished our love trip in the bedroom, Ram seriously asked me if I would join him now that his three months were over and he had to report to Bangalore for his posting.

'You deserve the best, Sandhya, come away with me.'

'What about Vinay, the family, my parents?' I questioned him.

'Leave them aside, are you happy with me?' he asked me point blank.

'Does it matter? I am always happy when you are around,' I answered him.

'Then it's fixed. I am booking tickets for both of us. We will be living in Bangalore. For some time there will be chaos. But after that no one will be bothered about where you are and what you're doing. We can live happily ever after!' He said it so casually.

'What about Vinay? He is a nice person. I hate to dupe him like this!'

He pulled me closer to him and hugged me tight. It was more like he had engaged me in a tight grip. It was hurting.

'Sandhya, don't even think of him. I don't mind killing him to get you, you are mine, mine alone . . .' The menacing way in which he said these words suddenly frightened me.

I wanted Ram, but Vinay was going to suffer because of me. Somehow Ram convinced me everything would be all right after some time.

I smiled and did my chores well the next day without even giving Vinay any clue about my plans. As he left for work, suddenly Vinay stopped near the doorway and looked at me saying, 'Sandhya I may not be able to give the you the moon but whatever is possible and within my reach I can do. I love you with all my heart!'

The way he said it melted my heart, tears ran down my face and out of the blue I hugged him tight. I just did not feel like letting him go.

After five minutes I relaxed my grip and he left, a happy man, for I could see the spring in his step, but my heart felt heavy.

Ram was watching me and my actions while drinking coffee in the hallway. We did not speak to each other, as the maid was present. I tried avoiding him and shut myself in the bedroom. Eventually he knocked. I slowly opened the door. 'Sandhya the flight is at 5.30 p.m., I am leaving for office and then from there I will be waiting for you at the airport. You'd better be there!' It was more of a statement than a request. He pulled me towards him and kissed me hard. It hurt. He left me and went away.

I sat in the living room staring blankly at the ceiling till the bell buzzed, bringing me back to my senses. It was the milkman. I took the two packets of milk he gave and placed them in the refrigerator. Suddenly I felt a huge burst of nausea sweep in. After vomiting, I felt drained and went back to my bedroom to lie down for some time. I wanted to go away with Ram, he was my passion, my dream come true and now suddenly I was scared, my safe cocoon was going to break, a secure compound was going to be shattered to satisfy my wild needs.

I absent-mindedly picked up my cellphone. But it was not mine, Ram had forgotten his cell. 'No problem,' I thought, 'I can give it to him when I meet him.' Now where was my cell? Suddenly an idea hit me and I searched for my name on his cellphone. I could not find it in his call list. I felt naughty and searched to see whether he had stored it as Darling, Sweetheart, Love, Girlfriend, GF, etc. I just could not find my name, so I typed my number, and was shocked. He had named me 'Time Pass'.

I slumped back on the bed. Time Pass! Was that what I was to him, all the sweet nothings, our lovemaking, joy rides was just that—time pass.

～

I was with Symala, my twin sister. I told her all about what had happened. My attempt at suicide and then coming back home, dejected. She was listening intently. I cried my heart out.

'I believed him and wanted to go away with him but I was just a small challenge to him! Nothing but "time pass"! To think I wasted all my time not looking at the real diamond . . .'

Symala consoled me. 'It was a good thing I came home first, and not Vinay. What's wrong with you? I was shocked to see your letter. Imagine if Vinay would have read it! Anyway forget Ram, good riddance! Actually I am shocked you even gave him a chance.'

I looked blankly at her.

'I got your test results . . .' she said. 'It is positive.'

I looked at her horrified. 'What? Positive!' I shouted.

Symala was a doctor. I had visited her clinic two days back because I was feeling very sick. Now with all my worries she told me that the results were positive.

'There now, why are you crying? It is for our good . . .'

I gaped at her. What was she thinking? How could she say 'it is for our good'?

'How can I face Vinay? How can I tell him about the baby? I'm myself not sure whose baby it is!'

'Just shut up, okay? Everyone makes mistakes. And similar to the one you've made, too! That does not mean the world has come to an end. And what are you telling me about this dying stuff? Better get yourself together and leave the thoughts of suicide to someone else! Be happy you're going to be a mother! I called Vinay and he was bursting with happiness so . . .' before she could complete her sentence, Vinay entered the room with gifts and chocolates and many more things. He was so happy! I was happy for him too. I forgot about Ram and took part in his happiness.

Symala stayed with me for a week or so. She was worried I might do something stupid again. Vinay was more than pleased with her assistance. My life changed again. I became more responsible and saw Vinay in a different light.

One night I had retired to the bedroom, citing a bad headache. I could not sleep though. So after half an hour I came out to get a glass of hot milk, hoping it would help me feel better. It was then that I happened to eavesdrop on my sister and Vinay's conversation.

'Thank you for coming in time,' he said to Symala.

'Any time Vinay, after all she is my sister!' I wondered where the conversation was leading.

'I was shocked to see the letter. I had no idea where she was and her phone was switched off. It was a good thing you called in at the right moment and I blurted out to you that she's left me. If you wouldn't have come immediately, I am sure I would have killed myself too! I really love her, you know, from the bottom of my heart.'

The way he had said it all melted my heart.

'I had tried calling her, but since her phone was switched off, I tried yours. What are you going to do about the baby?' she asked him in a low voice. I caught my breath. He knew! He'd come home early and seen my letter. And all the while I was thinking he was in the dark.

'What do you mean about the baby? It's mine, and that is the end of the topic! As for Ram, he is a closed chapter. I am going to make sure my second innings with Sandhya is going to be forever!'

By now I had begun to cry. I ran back to my room and closed the door softly. All this had happened within a week. Strange, wasn't it? Suddenly my cellphone rang. I answered— it was Ram. I cut him off and then on an impulse switched off my phone, took out the SIM card and broke it into two pieces. Vinay came in just then. He glanced at what I was doing. Without a word, he took the SIM, threw it into the dustbin and said, 'I shall get you a new number tomorrow. It is quite late, so you better go to sleep, mummy . . .' I loved the way he said that!

I showed him Ram's phone; he took that from my hand and flung it out of the window.

'As for that, it's settled and no more talking about it, darling.'

I put my head on the pillow. I'd learnt a lesson in that one week—don't feel bad if something is going wrong today, for tomorrow will always be a brighter day. Suicide is a word with two meanings, 'death' for some. But also 'think again'—'So Decide'. A split second can make a lot of difference.

# A Chapter, Closed

### SHALINI J. PILLAI

I saw Samira for the first time near my office corridor. As I was getting into the lift, she was standing there, flirting with some guy. Anybody would have noticed her, and so did I. As I passed, I couldn't help but check out her killer smile; she sure was killing that guy with it! She was plump but terrifically attractive. Her chiffon sari could not hide her gorgeous curves. Adding to that was her almost backless blouse. As a matter of fact, anything would have looked good on her. To my standards, her dressing was purely provocative and I defined it as 'vulgar'. But I presumed it might not be the same for any of the men in my office. To them, 'nothing' would have looked even better on her.

Later I learned that this was the very same girl my colleagues, both men and women, kept talking about. The difference was, men talked with desire and women with sheer envy.

Samira was hosting one of our musical reality shows. She made headlines every single day inside our channel. Wherever I went, I either heard about her or saw her on one of those previewing monitors installed on every floor of our office building. And there was never a need for any external audience when she was hosting a programme!

The first time we ever talked was when she was introduced to me by my colleague who produced her show. We were looking for an anchor for our new live phoning programme, someone who could talk voraciously and catch the attention of the audience. And Samira came to my mind instantly. But my boss said that out loud. 'Why don't we ask that girl to do it, what is her name? Samira . . . right? I couldn't just stop smiling and, full of envy, said to myself, 'God, this girl is so much in demand!'

We formally approached her and she agreed. And from then on I began my acquaintance with Samira.

Samira was a producer's anchor. She was one of the best anchors I have worked with. I have always tried to make all the anchors feel comfortable with me. But it was different with her. She knew exactly what I wanted. I just had to give her a clue and she used to set the floor on fire. I believed our wavelengths matched (at least professionally) even though I had to make a few compromises. I was tempted more than once to go and adjust her dress to appear appropriate but considering the TAM rating, I preferred silence. With a successful show in my pocket (without much of my own effort) I received smiles of satisfaction from my superiors. I was at ease. However, two things still bothered me. I hadn't yet figured out a way to control the crowd assembling in front of the Production Control Room during her show. Nor could I control the telephone which went wild every day, at least half an hour before and after her show was aired!

Everything was going on well until that fateful night. I had invited a few friends home for my birthday party. Samira was one of them. We had a great time with music and dance and, of course, the inevitable drinks. Now I have friends with all sort of drinking habits, varying from hard core to medium, slight, and social drinking. Being an amateur in drinking myself, Samira took me by surprise. She was a hard core drinker at the very age of nineteen and it has only been a year since she was even considered to be an adult! So she wasn't really drunk even after quite a few glasses of vodka. Looking at me, and guessing what I had on my mind, she said, 'I know what you are thinking,' and she winked at me with that same smile that killed most of the men in my office. I smiled back. But in my heart I almost felt guilty and responsible for this little girl.

Towards the end of the party, my guilt was obvious. She was completely drunk. But her zest for dancing and enjoying life did not slack. Her speech was still clear. Finally, exhausted, she came and sat next to me on the couch where I had already retired. Bored by my silence, she started a conversation with a typical question, 'Do you have a boyfriend?'

Unsure about if I should respond, I said, 'Yes and no.'

Confused she asked again, 'Now what does that mean?'

I said, 'It's complicated.'

Irritated, she continued probing, 'Now what is this complication?'

To that I replied, 'There is a guy. We like each other, but our families don't approve.'

'Oh, okay! That's all? Now what is so complicated about that? If both of you love each other then let the families go to hell, it's as simple as that. God, you are such a coward. Grow up!'

'Ya, of course, now I should learn things from you "Miss Grown-up",' I said mockingly.

I definitely didn't want to go further with this topic, so in order to distract her, I asked her the same question, 'Why don't you tell me? Do you have any crush from college? Or what about a boyfriend?'

'Yes I do!' came the instant reply.

'That's cool, who is he? Your classmate? Or senior?'

'Nope, he works for your channel!' she replied with a sly smile. Her face lit up.

I realized my tiredness was diminishing. 'Wow! Now this is interesting! Tell me more. Do I know him?'

'You might know him, try guessing,' she winked again with that same smile.

Now I was very excited with this new game. I started guessing all the people whom I knew from my channel, all my colleagues, producers, assistant producers, crew, the new interns, anybody I could think of, even my seniors, but all in vain.

'C'mon tell me now, I give up,' I said, feeling impatient.

'But promise me you won't tell anybody,' she said with a serious expression.

'I promise. Now please tell!' I'd lost my patience.

'I am having an affair with your bureau head,' she stated.

'WHAT?' It took a few seconds for me to recover from the shock.

She smiled that same mysterious smile.

'Again, what?' I asked still not believing.

'Yes it's true, I am in love with him,' she said very casually with drunken excitement and happiness on her face.

'Samira, are you aware of what you are saying!' I yelled. 'Are you talking about the chief editor of the news bureau, Rajneesh Verma?' I yelled again.

'Yes that's my man!' Saying that she winked again.

I felt like fainting.

I was disturbed by the truth about the man I so much admired professionally and personally. He was a role model for many of us who had just begun our career. Our news bureau department was maintained very well by this man alone and he was also one of the best news anchors. Personally, he was my guide and a good friend. Often, I would seek his advice on work issues. Apart from that, he was also my literary critic. I used to show him all my scribbles and doodles because I believed nobody I knew could review a piece of art like he did. Such a gem of a man! Yet I forgot he was also a 'man'.

I confirmed with Samira again the next day. I was hoping that she would say that everything she told me last night was completely false, and under the influence of vodka. But she stuck to her story. She also detailed it out for me. It all began with a New Year event hosted by our channel, three months back. Samira was hosting it and Raj was in charge of the event. They had been working together for this event for days in advance. I wasn't surprised when Samira told me that before she knew it, she'd fallen for Raj.

He was admirable and she was a charming teenager. A spark could have been ignited. But an affair was definitely a shock. Just to get a grip on the situation I asked her one more question. This time I didn't feel shy or awkward. I just had to ask her. 'How far has your relationship, affair or whatever . . . gone? You know what I mean . . .'

To that she answered very seriously, 'I know what you mean . . . I have been to his house a few times when his wife was away.'

My heart sank due to many reasons. And suddenly I remembered his wife, who was also a good friend of mine, chief producer of the art and entertainment department, Shalini Verma.

I was very angry with Samira and Raj at the beginning. I felt bad about everything I had heard. The very thought of it made me feel uncomfortable. Yet I didn't tell anybody about this. Not because I promised Samira, but just because I didn't want to think about it or even be associated with it. I felt awkward talking to Samira or Raj. I tried to avoid them. But since Samira and I worked together that wasn't possible.

The show went on as usual. She would come, give her best shot, enchant the audience with her smile, and leave. Detecting a behavioural change, one night after the show Samira came to my cabin. I was alone and wrapping up work for the day. She said, 'I know what you are thinking. You might find all of this wrong. But I love him and can't live without him. I have very few friends, and I consider you as one. That's the reason I told you everything. Please don't hate me for this.' She looked serious and her smile was missing.

Instead I smiled and assured her, 'We will always be friends, Samira.'

I was no longer angry with Samira, because I wasn't sure whether she was a victim or the culprit. All sorts of questions started popping up in my mind. A nineteen-year-old falling in love with a thirty-nine-year-old married man with a four-year-old kid is something far more than I could take or understand.

Was this pure love or pure lust? I couldn't stop wondering.

Did she really love him or was it just the infatuation of a teenager?

She was very talented and smart and naturally attractive. At such a young age, success and fame were already marching towards her. And on this path she had stumbled upon this newfound love which blinded her to reality.

And what about him? He was a person with a bigger history. He had married the woman he loved in his youth, even after their families had disapproved.

Shalini was a wonderful woman, a committed wife and a dedicated mother. She was older than him. I felt she was far more talented and mature than him. Initially, just after their marriage, they worked in the same department. Later on, she compromised her career for their only child. When she returned to work, she switched to the entertainment department from news, where the workload was less, in order to spend more time with their child.

Samira and Rajneesh Verma's affair continued smoothly for few more months. I got used to the situation. And Samira and I never discussed this topic again.

But here and there, rumours started surfacing about them. Some of the staff claimed that they had spotted them together in the city. Just as I was about to warn Samira, major gossip about them exploded.

One morning, as I entered my cabin, a colleague pulled me aside and murmured, 'Did you hear about your anchor, Samira?'

Her question made me anxious and my heart started beating fast as I asked, 'What?'

'She and our bureau chief were caught in his car in the office parking area last night. One of our night-duty cab drivers is the witness . . .' she murmured so low that half of what she said was inaudible.

'Rubbish!' I shouted. She was taken aback. 'I just told you what I heard,' she spat out in anger and left.

Soon the news spread like wild fire throughout the channel. People were now more interested in the internal news than the news around the world. Everyone was talking but no one talked openly. That was the culture of the channel.

I worried about Samira but, as always, she surprised me. She seemed very little affected by this. I have always respected Samira for her professionalism. No matter what was happening in her personal life, she never let it affect her on-screen presence.

That day after the shoot I asked her, 'Samira, are you okay?'

'I am cool. You just chill. My skin is like that of a rhino!' She winked while saying so.

I definitely agreed.

I never ever considered asking Raj about this although in my mind I have asked him a thousand questions. But one day as I was sitting in my office canteen having tea, he just came and sat in front of me.

'Hello, young lady! Very busy nowadays!' he exclaimed cheerfully.

'Yaa, was busy with shooting a new programme,' I replied with a fake smile.

'No new write-ups?' he asked.

'Haven't found the time.' Saying so I just looked at him. I couldn't help but ask him the same question I asked Samira, 'Are you okay?'

He replied with the same cheerful smile, figuring out what I meant. 'You know me. I am fine and happy as always.'

In my mind I shouted, 'Hell no, I don't know you at all!' I wondered how he could act as if nothing unusual had happened in his life.

'I know what you are thinking, my dear friend . . .' He was starting to say something when I rudely interrupted him with a question he'd never expected from me.

'Do you love your wife?' I asked, overcome by emotions.

'Excuse me?' he asked, still surprised, his expression turning serious.

'It is a simple question, do you?'

He answered with silence. That is when I regained my senses and felt foolish for asking him this question, which was none of my business. I was just going to apologize and ask him to ignore what I had just asked, when he replied, 'I love another woman.'

I was the one silent this time because I didn't know how to respond. He had answered my question. Then he got a call and he left.

Soon the news of their affair was gaining way more popularity than it deserved. It had reached such an extent that people started discussing them openly, breaking all the traditions. Everybody came to know, families got involved. At last, to bring the situation under control, the management had to interfere. Many meetings were held secretly by the superiors regarding how to suppress this issue. And finally it was decided that Samira should not be associated with the channel any further.

I still never understood the logic behind this decision. But I sure felt it wasn't fair. Both were equally responsible. How come one person alone was being punished? She was asked to leave the channel premises soon after the meeting. She was also asked not to have any communication with the channel, which I still find absurd. I was angry with the management. After all, how far could they control people? They could never restrict Samira and Raj from seeing each other outside the office. Nor could they repair the damage Raj and Shalini's marriage faced. I tried to console myself with the thought that the management had taken this decision to prove the point that 'infidelity is not acceptable', at least in the office premises, although it was none of their business.

Ultimately, I was the one who suffered due to this fiasco. My show's TAM rating suffered tremendously. I could not find anyone to replace Samira.

I never got a chance to say goodbye to Samira in person. I tried calling her many times. She would not answer. Then I texted her saying I felt sorry for her. She replied, 'I will bounce back.'

After this incident I rarely saw Shalini. Nor did I call her. Partially, I felt guilty for not telling her when I had come to know about this. Everyone in the office looked at her with pity. There was even one set of gossip blaming her for her husband's infidelity. She cared less, she talked lesser. She came, she did her work and she left.

There is nothing that time can't heal. As days went on things got back to normal. People found new interesting topics to discuss. After all, this is a channel. People believed in staying up-to-date.

Of course, I still suffered. My show never regained the position it once enjoyed. But I have moved on.

I decided never to get emotionally involved in any other person's business. A lesson I learned which proved very useful in the future.

After a few months, I was surprised to get a call from Samira. She sounded very happy. She called to inform me that she was going to host the new season of a very famous musical reality show, in another top channel. It was indeed a great opportunity. I felt happy for her and wished her luck. She talked for nearly an hour. She updated me about the new happenings in her life, but she didn't mention anything about Raj. Maybe she deliberately avoided that topic, thinking it would make me feel uncomfortable. Maybe everything came to an end as soon as she stepped out of the office. I didn't ask, I didn't want to know.

For me it was a chapter closed.

# That Girl

### YAMINI PUSTAKE BHALERAO

I did not know her name. Neither did I know what she looked like. To me, she was just another rumour buzzing through the gossip-laden corridors of my hostel. She was 'that girl' who had been sent by her middle-class, conservative parents to study, from a remote town in another state, like some 250 other girls living in the same hostel.

I was pursuing my graduation in a college nearby. The proximity to the college was the only reason why I was staying in a decrepit, rat-infested and filthy building along with twenty other batch mates. Apart from books, notes, clothes and accessories, gossip was also shared by us, with a dollop of homemade pickles. It was our favourite pastime in the absence of television and Internet—sharing rumours, most of which were the fictional work of many creative minds. But sometimes it would be the truth, told in confidence to a friend or a colleague, which travelled in hushed voices from one room to another, before the conversation was even over. And that is how I heard about her.

That girl, who was a new admission and had made a boyfriend already! That girl, who went on bike rides and dates with him. That girl, who suddenly looked disturbed and worried. That girl, who was seen crying silently in the dim-lit corner of the corridor. That girl, who was having a nervous breakdown. That girl, whose worst nightmare had come true.

'So that girl collapsed today.' I remember a friend telling me. 'She was going out with this guy . . . she slept with him and he filmed her!' she continued. Well, this was something new! We had heard of many affairs gone horribly wrong. Every now and then, some boy would create a ruckus in front of the hostel, which was followed by name calling and threatening. But this was the first time such a horrible thing had happened to one of the girls. Suddenly, everyone wanted to know what was up with that girl.

'That girl is becoming delirious. She keeps crying. We have called her local guardians, her friends, doctor . . . but no one can console her,' one of her concerned seniors said the next day. While we all felt for her, every girl was grateful to God that it wasn't her or any of her friends or sisters. And as that thought passed, so did the interest in the news. We all resumed our lives after collectively wondering about her fate and scrutinizing how and where she went wrong.

It's not easy to leave home for the very first time, and live in a strange new city—without parents guiding you at every step and without the cocoon-like comfort of home. The loneliness, the tight budget, the freedom, the excitement and eagerness to experience emotions unchecked are some of the key ingredients of hostel romances. Some boys and girls are sincerely looking for companionship and love. But some others have different priorities; some are looking for free recharge vouchers, long bike rides, parties and branded clothes despite tight budgets. Some are looking for sexual escapades, away from the disciplinary and conservative eyes of their parents, and the bragging rights in front of friends. The permutations and combinations of all these intensions either lead to love, or to heartbreaks, betrayals, rage or, like in that girl's case, a suicide attempt.

One night, after she gathered enough courage, she called her parents to make the confession. And a few minutes later, she jumped from the second-floor balcony. Maybe she was too delirious to realize that a fall from such a height might not kill her, but injure her gravely; the consequences of which she might have to bear for the rest of her life (worse than death, some might argue). Or maybe she just had no more strength to go through it all . . . I never figured it out.

But she took the plunge that fateful night. By the time I came to know about it and reached the spot from where she jumped, she had been rushed to the hospital. I looked down . . . and the only remnant of the incident stared back at me. A lone sandal, lying at an awkward angle on the hard concrete floor.

She came back after a few days, with a broken femur and some other minor injuries; and a harrowed mother in tow, who had left behind an equally jolted father and her household to nurse her daughter. She slowly made a physical recovery and we spotted her every now and then learning to walk again with help from her mother. The scars faded away as well. And so did the incident from our memories.

Soon 'that girl' was nothing more than a stale rumour whose shelf life was over and which had been replaced by another spicy fresh piece of gossip. While just a few days ago, all we talked about was that girl, now none of us even bothered to visit her and sit by her side. We were mere spectators, who watched a free show of devastation of a girl's life, and we moved on as soon as it was over, not even bothering to look back, let alone help to clean the mess. After all it was not our mess.

I wonder now, what turmoil the poor girl must have faced. Her only fault was that she was naïve and not cautious enough and trusted a boy blindly. And she paid a big price for that. She was scarred mentally and physically for life. The humiliation of your body being filmed and that video being shared shamelessly by lusting men, like a piece of cake. The guilt of putting your parents through so much pain. The fear of being an outcast .Those constant, unsympathetic, judgemental stares from each and every direction.

Was it she who failed her parents and society, or was it the other way around? Shouldn't it have been the boy who filmed her, and his friends who watched that video, who should have been ashamed? Shouldn't it be us, who failed to look beyond her as a rumour, who should be ashamed?

Years have passed, and I shamefully admit that now I don't remember her face, or even her name. But I still remember peering down from the second floor balcony to see a lone sandal lying awkwardly on the concrete floor. Used and then neglected. A vision which sums up the story of that girl for me. And of many more like her, about whom I read in newspapers every now and then.

That girl is a lesson for each one of us, of how things could go wrong. Of how lust and betrayal are the daggers sometimes hiding underneath the pretence of love and trust. Of how our impotence as a society to stand by the victims of sexual crimes, are in fact, an encouragement to the predators. Of how humanity is fast disappearing as we become numb to incidents which have rattled someone's life.

If only I could apologize to that girl . . .

# The Love That Made Me

## AADITI DHYANI

Growing up in a broken family, I had changed in more ways than one.

I was a recluse. I hardly smiled. My grades were average and even though people around me believed in my potential, I entirely lacked incentive.

Always being in the shadow of my father's overbearing criticism had made me devoid of any wish of being worthy of success. Of love. And especially of admiration.

I was not entirely alone. I had my mother. And in the days that I felt like ending my life, she was the only solace I felt I had. And the only person I felt emotionally attached to. That was until the time he came into my life.

He was like a human tornado who took over my life with so much exuberance oozing out of him that the first time we met, I almost considered punching him.

I was already having a bad day. My teachers had complained to my father about my lack of concentration. Everybody knew I sometimes zoned out. It was not exactly a shock to my father either. But like every time, I was pulled up for it. When I reached my tuition place that day, I was already hyperventilating. As the class finally ended, I had annoyed my tuition teacher as well. Terrific.

I was worried about my mother's reaction and my father's subsequent anger which he will let out on her. I did not want my mother to interfere. She always ended up receiving more insults from my father than I would have initially been subjected to.

Lost in thought, I didn't see where I was going and realized it too late. I had already bumped into someone. I started mumbling half-hearted apologies and tried to get away as soon as possible. I was embarrassed. It was one thing to be caught daydreaming and totally another to just bump into a stranger while doing so! I hadn't noticed that in the process, I had spilled my books on the road. Awesome.

He bent down and started picking up my books while I just stood there looking like an idiot.

I was startled when he stood up and smiled at me. Like a genuine I-am-so-happy kind of smile. Next moment he held out his hand.

'I am Hamid. It's my first day here. I know you from your music classes. Though I think you hardly know me. So?'

At that 'so', I finally regained my common sense. I hardly talked to people I knew, let alone strangers. And here was this guy who knew so much about me and was behaving like we were already friends. Yeah, right.

Shoving general courtesy aside, I kept my hand stiffly at my side and scowled. That was the expression I usually used to ward off unwanted attention. But Hamid was not one to be so easily shooed off.

'You don't smile, do you? Is it ugly?' He grinned.

I started seething. How dare he comment on my smile or the lack of it for that matter!

'I do smile. Just not for stupid strangers,' I replied.

'But I am no stranger. So tell me, can I walk with you? I live in the same area and I really don't like walking alone.'

That was exactly what I wanted. To gather my thoughts and make new excuses for being late. Because this little accidental chitchat with him had cost me precious minutes.

Without giving him a second glance I started moving forward.

'Oye. Wait for me!' He started walking by my side. My scowl hadn't worked so I thought of another idea. To ignore him totally.

'Are you not going to talk at all? It's a long way, it'll be easier to pass time if we were conversing.'

Getting no response from me, he started humming a tune to himself. It was my favourite song. So when he showcased his talent in mixing two totally different tones in one, I was tempted to correct him. But I refrained.

As we reached my house, I parted ways.

'See you tomorrow?' he asked.

I just went on without replying.

The next day was the same. After class, I tried to hurry off. Though after my behaviour the previous day, I didn't expect him to follow me.

But Hamid was waiting for me. Acting like it was nothing unusual, he started walking beside me. I had to give it to him—he was resilient. This walk then became his routine.

He didn't try talking to me after that first day but whenever I glanced his way, I could see a satisfied smile on his lips.

Finally, after four weeks of arrogance, I was overcome by curiosity.

'Why do you always have a smile plastered on your face?'

'People tell me I look handsome while smiling. And really, who wouldn't want to look great in front of girls!'

'There aren't many girls around here, you do know that, right?'

'One is enough for me,' he countered.

At that, I couldn't help smiling. And he started his iconic babble.

'You know you are not taxed for smiling, yet?'

'Yes. I do,' I frowned.

'So why don't you try smiling a bit more? A smile a month is seriously wrong.'

I didn't reply. He may have had reasons for smiling always. I didn't.

'Okay! Don't get so sulky. I was just kidding. So are we friends now?'

'I don't know.'

'Come on! I made you smile. I earned it!'

'Okay.'

'Okay, we are friends or okay, you are annoying?'

'Both.'

My reply made him sulk. And his expression was so cute that I started laughing. He looked at me, surprised.

'Now we are definitely friends!' Thus he sealed our bond.

I failed to resist him. He was so full of hope and light that even the eternal night of my life was starting to get affected.

As the days progressed, I got to know more about him. He was an only child of an army officer. His mother had died at a young age and he hardly remembered her. I in turn told him about my mother.

Sometimes we bunked class. It was his idea that we roam around, and be explorers.

'Bunking is healthy. You are already a nerd. How much more can you mug?'

'I don't mug. And where will we go, if we do miss the class?'

'Let me show you Hamid's haven.'

'There is no such thing as that.' I cut him off.

It was another of his quirks—naming things as he pleased.

'There is, dumbo. Just come along.'

He never liked it if I didn't believe him. To humour him, I followed. Finally, we stopped at a forest.

'What is this place?' I asked.

'This once used to be a bamboo farm. Nobody comes here now. It's secluded.'

'Okay.'

'You don't like it?' he sounded disappointed.

'No. I like it. It's peaceful here.'

'Yeah. It is. That's why I come here whenever I feel like being alone.'

'I thought you were the kind of person whose life was perfect,' I mused aloud.

'Nobody's life is perfect, mine definitely isn't. Perfection is overrated. How will we grow better if we were perfect already? And problems exist in each person's life. It's on you how much you weigh them against your happiness.'

That struck a chord. I had decided to let my problems consume my life completely, he had decided to live with them and not let them hinder his liveliness.

Considering my expression, he came closer.

'Try being the girl you are. Not what your problems have made you.'

As I sat down on the grass, he began talking: 'The first thing I noticed when I saw you singing was the sadness in your eyes. And that surprised me. Because whenever I asked anybody about you, the response was similar. "Try staying away from her. She won't think twice before insulting you for just being nice to her." But I was intrigued. And that was when I decided that I'll try getting through your facade. And I did.'

He again sounded very smug. I shoved him against the tree and he started laughing. After a minute I joined in too.

At that moment I knew I liked him. More than I'd ever liked someone. He was everything I needed. Sensitive. Funny. Caring. He could make me laugh when all I wanted to do was cry. He understood me. He had told me numerous times, 'You could be great. If you just stopped being the symbol of world grief.'

I felt hope surge within me. I didn't want to fail him. So I tried to improve. I studied. I worked hard. And I started paying less heed to my father's taunts.

I decided to be happy. When my mother asked me the reason behind my sudden good spirits, I tried to be nonchalant about it. Hamid was my secret, and I wanted to keep it that way for now.

We started frequenting his spot, which he had now named after both of us. We found that the zigzagging and interlocking bamboo leaves had grown to form a green canopy. We loved it!

Hamid decided to put up a swing on those branches. We installed it on the strongest branch we could find. We took turns on it. I loved the feeling of being airborne, being free, even if for a few minutes. And Hamid never grew tired of waiting and watching me go even higher.

Months passed. The year was almost coming to an end. We had our exams and we agreed to halt our escapades.

That was when I knew what missing someone felt like. I always had this urge to just see him once, even if for a few seconds, to talk to him. But I stayed put.

On the last day of our exams, my friends had organized a party. Usually, I wasn't allowed to go. And I would not mind missing such outings. But this time I wanted to enjoy myself. So I went ahead with my plan to not ask my father. I just told my mother. After I returned, he was already waiting. Somehow he knew. He slapped me and slammed me against the wall. I couldn't control myself any further so I lashed out at him. When he regained his composure, he came after me. I ran out of the door. I had nowhere to go and I was angry. So I went to the one place I knew, just wanting to spend a few hours alone.

After a few minutes, I heard someone approach. I looked up and saw him. He had the most peculiar expression on his face. He looked concerned but there was also a trace of trepidation. As if I would bite him if he said a word wrong. It was almost comical to see such an unusual emotion on his face. I started laughing.

He was here. Why? How? I didn't know. It was a relief so exquisite that I couldn't understand whether to laugh or cry. He came closer and sat down beside me. For the first time he was silent. I kept my head on his shoulders and cried. My tears started soaking through his shirt but he didn't mind. He took my hand in his and started counting on my fingers.

Usually, I did not like being touched. But that day, I drew comfort from his strength. His shoulders provided me stability. I felt safe. And strangely whole. He was my one refuge from the world of pain that enveloped me.

After calming down a bit, I asked him about it.

'I am counting the number of tears you are wasting over someone who doesn't care about you. If you are crying like this for him, you ought to cry me a river some day.'

'Why?' I was amused.

'I may have to leave some day. I can't always be around you.'

'Why?'

'Because my father could get transferred. We could go to different colleges. Or any number of things could happen.'

For the first time, I saw him agitated.

'But that's not necessary. I'll take admission in whichever college you go to. So we could be together.'

'Never destroy a chance at a better future of your own will. Not even for me. Or anybody. You should do whatever you want.' He sounded angry.

'Don't worry. We'll be together. No matter what. Even if we go to different colleges, we can still meet, right?' I asked.

'We will. But that is the future. Let's not rush it.'

With that, he stood up. He held out his hand for me and I happily took it. We walked like that the rest of the way. He dropped me at my home. And I bade him goodbye.

Never once did I imagine that it would be the final time I would see his face.

For the next month, I was grounded. I asked my friend to tell this to Hamid. After my term ended, the first thing I did was go to our place. It was still the same though it appeared a bit forlorn. I idly wondered why Hamid hadn't taken care of it. I waited for an hour for him to arrive, but he didn't. Maybe he had stopped coming here. I didn't think it was possible. This was our safe haven. Our spot.

A week passed in this manner. I waited every day, my hope wearing thin, for him to arrive. He never did.

Then came my birthday. I was in denial. I still wanted him to show up. As I sat waiting, I heard a rustle. Expecting to find him smiling down at me, I was disappointed to see his friend coming through. As I stood up, I noticed the package he was holding.

'Hey. Hamid told me to give this to you.'

He held out the package and I took it. After thanking him, I asked him whether Hamid was fine.

'Oh, yes. He's fine. You should just open the note first. I'll let you be.'

With that he left and I was alone. There was a note stuck to the gift. I opened it.

'Happy birthday. Promise me not to cry, whatever happens.'

After reading it twice to confirm, I was filled with a sense of foreboding.

I opened the package. Inside was the most beautifully carved bracelet I had ever seen. It was wooden, inlaid with crystals that spelled 'smile'. I loved bracelets. Marvelling at how much he knew about my likes, I opened up the letter that was tucked inside the box. It was his sloppy handwriting, no doubt.

As I began reading, my happiness started crumbling under the weight of the blows that I was receiving through his words. I felt myself choking and I started taking deep breaths to stop myself from breaking down.

He had left. His father had been posted to Leh. Hamid had been shifted to a boarding school in his native place. He had asked me to promise not to cry, but at that moment I was finding it hard to keep my composure. Without his presence, I wanted to let go of everything I had strived to change in me. But he had asked me for something in return.

'Promise me to never go back to the way I met you. You don't realize your smile's value. It's wonderful. Don't make some other guy force it out of you again. Because you know there's just one Hamid. So don't let him take my place. Make a different place for him. More special. Fall in love. Be happy. And when you can't find any reason to smile, just wear the bracelet. And remember me. Hopefully, I gave you enough memories to make you happy. I wish I could stay. I loved you. I don't know how you felt about me, but I wish I meant enough to you for you to never break the promise you made me. The world is a better place when you smile.'

After reading it so many times that I had it memorized, I folded the letter and kept it back along with the bracelet. I didn't cry. That was the promise I had made. And he meant the world to me at that time. So how could I refuse him the only thing he had asked for? I knew I loved him. I regretted not telling him sooner.

Everything happens for a reason. Sometimes the journey proves to be more important than the destination. Not every story has a happily ever after. Our story is still etched in my heart and maybe in his too. Our time together was short. But full of great memories.

His love showed me a new hope. A brighter window to look at the world. I cannot imagine how my life would have shaped out had it not been for him. His arrival was a blessing. I overcame my pain. I became a better person.

Love is all about giving hope when there is no reason to be optimistic. And being the best we can be for the person we love.

# Pages from a Writer's Life

### SHAMITA HARSH

In the cosy town of Dehradun the colours are vivid, the sky is blue in the purest form of the hue and the air is pollution-free to a large extent. The community is knit closely in the tapestry of the society and a majority of the population shares a love for reading or writing. Amidst hordes of small-town dwellers, in the heart of the valley surrounded by the Shivaliks, I lived with my parents and sister, long before it all began.

I had always been a dreamer. I think it had something to do with the place, and the people too. It moulded me into a vessel that could take the form of any thought, that could contain any dream.

Early on in my life, I learnt that it is difficult to become a writer. Once you have gone through the ordeal of penning your thoughts, you do not realize that there is much that lies beyond that stage. It is only half the journey. It is necessary to understand what happens in a writer's life, I always told myself.

I did not know that my curiosity would lead me one day to become the subject of my inquisitiveness.

I transformed into a writer. It was a gradual process. Right from my school days I had had an inclination towards poetry and prose. I devoured novels by the day even if my diet as a scrawny kid remained minimalistic. I stayed active but my thoughts would often wander into a space very different from the present time. This space had become like a second home and I would drift back and forth. From now to then, from here to there, I would jump time and again.

My family loved to travel and my parents made sure no vacation was spent home in idle musings of the infamous holiday homework. So I discovered many hidden places in India and while I was at it, I developed a habit of keeping a journal. The journal would store the feelings of a teenager, the rebellious kind of secrets that I wouldn't want to share with anyone. I would write and lock away my feelings, away from the reach of my family or friends. It was a part of me that I didn't want to share, didn't want scrutinized by anyone.

Over time, I developed a habit of spinning stories. And while I would be at it I would be transported to the world which I was writing about—where the sounds were the only music I wanted to hear, where the visions were only the dreams that I wanted to see. In these stories I began to paint my words on a canvas that had every shade splashed across its length and breadth.

At the age of twelve, I finished the first draft of what would later become my first book. I had forced all my friends to write with me, but they weren't half as crazy. One afternoon, as my principal finished his lunch break, I went and showed him the book. He seemed pleased; the kind of pleased teachers are when their student does something well. Now when I look back at that smile he gave me when he said, 'You have done a great job!' I remember not quite understanding what he had meant.

Years later, I was in my second year of graduation in mass communication when my teacher called me aside for a little chat. She had helped me write a few columns for the local newspaper. She discussed my latest assignment and then told me on the second floor's corridor: 'You should write a book.'

My first reaction was: I laughed. She looked at me with her head tilted to one side and since she was four inches shorter than me she looked almost animated when she did that. She smiled and said, 'Don't be afraid. Stop being afraid. Just believe.'

That day I had an epiphany. I had always ranted about dreaming of being a writer, of hoarding books for a living, for sharing stories with the world and now someone had shown an interest in my dream. All of a sudden, the clouds of doubt descended on me, like I suppose they descend upon every writer before they are about to start something new. But I just heard my mentor's voice, one word floated in the air and echoed in my ear: BELIEVE! And well, I did just that.

For hours in a day, I would lock myself in a room only to resurface for meals. I would attend college but the moment I would get back, I would shut my door and just bleed over the keyboard. The words spilled out just like water gushing after the gates of a dam had been opened.

My room was full of storyboards where I would pin up notes and character sketches. I would read extensively. I would breathe the smell of my books every day, imagining what it would be like to have it printed in my hand one day, a book that had my name on it. In those dreams I cruised through my writing journey. I did not know then that I would be unleashing a monster inside me, for I had good days and bad ones too. My mood swung with the mood of the story, the pace of the story. There were days my mind just wouldn't budge. I ate little, slept even less. I had nightmares of not finishing my manuscript and I would wake up drenched in sweat on a cold winter morning.

I would get lost in between conversations, drift away in my story. I began carrying my not-so-light laptop that belonged to my father; I had taken charge of for the time being. Any moment an idea would seize me and I would sit on the edge of the seat in class and begin typing. There were moments when I speeded home on my two-wheeler to write. There were even times when I awoke in the middle of the night to write. And you know what they say about that: you never have to change what you write waking up in the middle of the night.

And then in less than three months I had completed the first draft. The tough part began then, as I juggled exams with editing. It was the most excruciating pain I had felt in my life. Slashing away the same lines I had written so passionately.

But only half the journey had been completed until now. The sea of publishers still needed to be waded through, especially with no shore in sight. I must have contacted almost 200 publishers. To keep track of all calls, meetings, emails and correspondence became a part-time job with no timings. To explain all that and my phone bills to my parents was a pickle.

Either a publisher was too rude, or too good. While the former I could somehow deal with, the latter made me doubt: why is he being so good to me? There must be something fishy, right?

Somehow I found one. It hadn't been easy, the roller-coaster of acceptance and rejections, but I managed to resurface.

After debating and contemplating unto eternity, I decided to publish my book *The Creepy Cuties* with cyberwit net.

Like I had planned, I signed the contract on the last date of my teenage days. It helped me strike off the last thing on my bucket list of things to do before I finished that phase of my life. And there below, 'Climb a tree; learn to ride a Scooty . . . etc.' was . . . 'Write my book' which I cut off with much delight in my heart.

On the morning of my twentieth birthday I woke up as an author. Some final cuts and the cover image were still being worked upon, but I knew the deed was done.

It would take another three months for the author's copies to arrive at my doorstep.

On 5 December 2013, the consignment arrived. The very first thing I did after ripping the package open was to smell the book. Something went off in my head, a checkbox neatly ticked: CHECK. It smelt right. (Unless you are a book person, you won't get this.)

From 1 January 2014 onwards, my book was available on e-commerce websites and was featured in the bookstores of my town. A book launch was organized amongst students of schools and colleges on 26 April 2014. Even though the turnout wasn't that big, I was overwhelmed as I stood on the stage addressing the youth of Dehradun. I realized how much in my life had changed, how much had happened since I had embarked upon this journey. A montage of moments swam before my eyes. I was out of breath by the time I ended delivering my keynote speech.

Children and parents, teachers and professors of various institutions surrounded me as I got off the stage. They wanted my autograph. It was while I was signing my name with little bits of personalized messages on their notebooks that I realized not too long ago that I had been like them, with millions of dreams in my eyes. As they asked me questions I answered patiently, always remembering that I would have wanted someone to answer my questions. I would have wanted someone to direct me. Before I left the venue they asked me to take pictures with them and I told them repeatedly not to call me 'Ma'am' for I was barely deserving of the stature they had given me.

I met my mentor a few days after the launch; she had been out on an assignment during the book launch and I had been shattered to hear that she wouldn't make it. These were the first words she spoke when we met: 'I told you, right? Just believe and you will see.'

# The Untied Shoelaces

DALIA JANE SALDANHA

'So, you really do not know how to tie your shoelaces?' asked the teacher in disbelief. The timid nod that followed as a reply forced her to turn back and sit down on her seat as she closed her eyes and massaged her temples with her right thumb and forefinger aggressively. Her expression displayed nothing more than tiredness. After a few seconds of what seemed like deep contemplation, she looked up and fixed her eyes on the shivering boy who refused to meet her gaze in fear. He stood there, in front of her, his tiny body trembling as the rest of his second-grade class looked on. His mother had written a special note to his class teacher which he had handed over to her that morning, little knowing that it would cause him so much humiliation in front of all his friends, who were now trying to suppress their laughter and giggles.

After what seemed like an eternity to him, his teacher broke the silence and beckoned him towards her. He lifted one of his legs and placed it on a nearby stool. She untied his shoelaces and held both of them separately, one in each hand.

'Hold both the strings in such a way that they cross each other, place one of them inside the loophole that is formed now and pull as hard as you can, got it?'

The boy mumbled incomprehensively in return. She continued to teach him by making double loopholes with each of the strings and tying a knot in the end to ensure it did not come off. As she continued to explain and demonstrate this foreign technique to him, he whimpered and groaned silently. He did not understand anything he was being told. All his friends were laughing at him. His mother had made him appear like a fool in front of everyone and why shouldn't she? He was eight years old and he still did not know how to tie his shoelaces. He was a laughing stock, not a hero like Spiderman, whose action figure lay on his bedside table, looking all magnificent and bold. He studied the figure's expression every night, wondering when his time would come to show that he was not an outcast but a superhero too.

When would the day come when people would cry out his name and be reminded of the immense courage, bravery and strength he had exhibited at the time of adversity? He wished he could do something so great one day that people all around the world would chant his name in awe, as he soared over skyscrapers and mountains fighting for justice. He turned and looked at his teacher, who was still talking to him. But for now, he thought to himself, he was stuck learning how to tie his shoelaces.

～

His best friend looked on, not knowing what to do. Shrieks of laughter could be heard from behind her. As she was sitting in the first seat of the front row, she could observe the whole scene clearly. Her best friend was sobbing silently in embarrassment.

The teacher, who was growing increasingly impatient with every passing second, now began to scold him. His mind had wandered by then and he did not respond to her even after being called thrice. 'He is probably fantasizing about saving the world again!' thought the small-faced, curly-haired girl to herself. Only five minutes had gone by but it seemed like five hours to her. The teacher's crooked brow and wrinkled cheeks scared her. The way she glared at him in fury also scared her. Her face, her hair, her talk and, above all, her hard, muscly hand never failed to terrify her. The older lady looked at him like as if she was trying to suppress an uncontrollable urge to slap the little boy. The little girl stared at her Velcro shoes. She had worn them since kindergarten.

She, too, did not know how to tie shoelaces.

Every cell in her body wanted her to stand up and confess this secret to her teacher. She could not let her best friend be subjected to her teacher's wrath and their friends' teasing all alone. But she could not get herself to do it. She kept looking down, her face glowing with shame. She knew what she was doing was wrong but she was spineless. She had no guts. She was the most cowardly girl the face of the planet had ever seen.

～

It was a windy winter afternoon. The entire class was dispersed into the large, sandy playground that extended far and beyond the capacity of human sight. To the little girl, this was her personal desert. She loved making sand castles here. She loved sitting on the swings but never went too high as she was scared she would fall down and hurt herself. She never let people push her on the slide as she did not like people controlling what she could do easily on her own.

As she sat alone on the see-saw she saw her best friend running as fast as he could, across the field, twisting and turning his back as the other boys tried to chase and catch him. He was a fast runner and a skilled sportsman. She recalled the number of times he had requested her to play with him and the other boys, but his pleas always fell on deaf ears. It was not that she did not like running or even catching other people for that matter. She feared humiliation. She was scared that people would see how slowly she sprinted because of her flat feet and would mock her. They would call her a 'turtle'. She was always being teased for her furiously curly hair and the last thing she needed in her life at the moment was more name-calling.

As her mind wandered around these thoughts, a sweating and gasping little body sat on the other end of the see-saw. The little girl was taken aback as she suddenly rose up in the air. She heaved a sigh of relief as she peeped through her squinting eyes at the weary figure on the other end of the see-saw. He grinned at her mischievously. He loved doing this. He loved surprising her and watching her expression after that. It was not such a hard task either, as she was always in some other world, her head in between clouds. She twitched and turned at the sight of him. He knew she was hiding something from him. Her nose always turned red whenever she felt guilty, like Rudolph the Reindeer. After a few minutes of silent play, she finally opened her mouth.

'I have something to say to you,' she said softly.

'Yes?'

'I do not know how to tie my shoelaces, too.'

'Oh.'

'That's it? You're not angry with me?' she said, half relieved as if a heavy burden had been resting on her shoulders all this while and someone had happily volunteered to take it off her.

'Why would I be angry?' asked the boy inquisitively.

'Well, it's not fair that everyone in class made fun of you because you did not know how to tie your shoelaces. They should make fun of me as well, right?'

'Nah, that's fine. Let's just keep it to ourselves. We do not need other people to know our little secret.'

This time the little girl stared right at his face and grinned widely at him. So, he was not angry with her after all! Moreover, he was not even planning to tell on her. Well, of course he would not have spread her secret to the entire class. She was his best friend. Why would he ever do something like that? As her thoughts travelled like a train inside her mind, they suddenly stopped at their tracks. She needed to know one more thing from him. 'So do you know how to tie your laces now?'

'Yeah, my mother made me sit up all night and practise.'

The sound of a whistle was heard from nearby. That was their signal to line up to go to class as recess had now come to an end. While the girl joined the line, the boy walked towards the front as he was one of the shortest in the entire class. This fact never failed to depress him in a profound manner. Even his best friend was taller than him. In fact, she was the tallest girl in the entire class and maybe even the entire second-grade.

As he proceeded towards the front, his best friend caught up with him and whispered in his ear, 'Will you teach me how to tie my shoelaces?'

He looked at her face, filled with eagerness and insecurity. 'Sure, when, now?'

'Of course, not now, you monkey! We have to go back to class. How about tomorrow?'

'Tomorrow is the first day of the winter vacation, you donkey!'

'Oh. Okay. Then, how about after the vacation? Teach me how to tie my laces after school re-opens again in January. Is that okay?'

'Sure.'

With these words they parted and walked towards their respective places in the long line of sweaty second-grade children.

~

The parking lot was filled with shrieks, screams and a lot of laughter. The school had officially closed for the winter. As the children headed towards their buses they hugged and high-fived and said goodbye to each other. The entire atmosphere was rife with cheerfulness and excitement. As the little girl was about to reach her bus, which always parked itself near the rose garden, someone patted her on her shoulder. She turned back.

'Oh, it's you,' she told the little boy whose face beamed with the same naughty smile he had flashed at her earlier that day.

'Merry Christmas!' he wished her.

'Merry Christmas to you, too,' she replied with a buck-toothed smile.

'I don't celebrate Christmas,' he said matter-of-factly.

'Oh yeah. Safe journey though. You're going to Sri Lanka with your family, right?

'Yeah, we are leaving tomorrow morning.'

'Oh, cool! By the way, you do remember your promise, right?'

'Oh, goodness, of course I do.'

'Okay, please don't forget.'

'I won't'

'Bye.'

'Bye.'

He waved as he turned his back on her, walking towards his bus parked on the other end of the garden. She looked at his receding figure and smiled on the inside. They were going to be friends forever. She just knew it.

~

Whenever the little girl visited her father's ancestral house during the vacations, her daily life would be filled with fantasy and awe. She loved to watch the hens dote over their newly born chicks, the dogs refuse to eat leftovers and cats try to scratch her little brother. She also loved the way she got up every morning to the cock's crow and not to the sound of her Disney Princess alarm clock, the way she would help her grandmother milk the cows early in the morning and also the times she was forced to take a shower inside her outdoor bathroom which had no roof. But what she simply adored was to watch the moths that would visit her household at night. Every evening at eight, when the entire village would be in deep slumber, she would sit on her father's lap and watch the moths dance in circles around the light bulb flashing in the front porch. They were always in pairs or groups and would flap their wings rapidly as if it was their form of play. They always seemed so content, moving around the bulb. They got all the light and heat that they needed.

But at nine o'clock when her grandmother would switch off the light and put her to bed, the moths would go crazy and fly here and there recklessly. They would scatter away in a million different directions. They would act all crazy and their once beautiful ensemble would go haywire. The light bulb would not provide them with happiness any more. They would no longer find solace in each other's company. They would completely lose their peace and calm.

That was how the little girl felt right now. Lost, alone and confused. Her life was undergoing the greatest turmoil ever. It was like someone was sucking her down a black hole and there was no way out. She had to face the hard truth. She was being forced to confront the harsh demons of reality. Ever since she had heard the news that morning she had lost all sense of understanding. She could not register the fact that she would not meet him for the next ten years. Or twenty. Maybe, even, forever. She remembered his crooked, evil smile and his oily, well-combed hair. She recalled his maroon school sweater, always tied around his waist, filthy with dirt and mud. Why, did he, of all people have to go there at a time like this? It seemed like everyone knew what had happened to him except her. As the entire world crowded around him, she stayed behind, far and away. For the reporters he was a news story but to her, he was her best friend. Who knew water, which was the source of all life and health on earth could be equally responsible for robbing a person of these very qualities. Water also killed mercilessly. It separated families, friends and loved ones. Water, like the light of the bulb, falsely allured us, the moths of the world, to self-destruction.

'Children, I want you all to close your eyes for a minute and pray for the souls of his father and mother who passed away in last month's tsunami that struck Sri Lanka. Also, his brother in the second-grade who, thankfully, managed to survive this disaster will no more attend school here—he will go to live with his uncle in America. Please pray to God so that he is blessed with the strength to cope up with his loss and begin life afresh.' They were praying for his brother.

As a thousand pair of eyes shut gently during the first school assembly after the winter break, the mind of the little girl raced furiously. Her best friend had managed to physically survive the tsunami unscathed. However, her prayers had failed to protect him from the emotional wounds the death of his family had caused him. According to the newspaper and her school, her friend had been saved by an NGO volunteer along with another eight-year-old boy. The bodies of his father and seventh-grader brother were found on the shore after the waves had calmed down. For several days, his mother went missing and all hope of her being alive died down upon the sight of her lifeless body that was found a month later. Now, as he had no member of his immediate family left, he had to live with his uncle in the United States of America.

As she pondered over these thoughts she wondered how much of it was actually true. She only knew what was being told to her. Who knew how he was actually rescued? Who knew how he had felt upon seeing the huge waves towering over the whole city? Had he felt scared? Had he cried when he found out about his family? Was he happy about leaving for the US? Above all, would he miss her? These were all good questions but their answers, like her life now, were filled with silence.

~

'So you really do not know how to tie your shoelaces?' asks her friend in disbelief. The little girl, at whom the question is directed, is not so little any more. Her hair is no more curly, but silky straight courtesy the wonders of modern technology. Her once baby skin is now filled with pimples and her rabbit teeth are adorned with metallic braces. The girl just giggles shyly in reply. The friend joins in the laughter, shaking her head simultaneously. 'Want me to tie them for you?' she asks. She receives a nod as an answer. As she watches her friend bend over to tie the laces for her, she recalls that day, eight years ago, when someone else had been asked the exact same question. She had watched him silently as he endured ridicule. She had been so scared, so frightened, so timid. That day she had not wanted to stand up for herself or for her friend. But now, she has changed. Not only physically, but mentally as well. She admits her fears out loud.

She does not think twice before saying how she actually feels. She does not care what people think about her. For our existence here on earth is defined by small and special moments. Nobody is aware of what is going to happen the very next minute. Life is too short to spend in silence and cowardice. Time goes by and she knows, one day, he will come back to fulfil his promise to her. She knows he would never let her down. But until then, the string of memories that they shared together will hang loose across the soles of her heart.

*Dedicated to my friend A. Rao whose parents and brother passed away in the 2004 tsunami.*

# We the People

ANJALI KHURANA

*I don't crib, complain, and curse any more. Each time I recall this twenty-minute interaction with a stranger, the soreness of my problems subside automatically. I'm sure you'll experience the same.*

On a boring Sunday afternoon, the bug of being unwanted and unmarried bit me hard and I decided not to turn a blind eye towards my loneliness, I decided to go to a place full of people. Marine Drive came to my mind. I have a huge circle of friends and they are just a phone call away but I decided to learn to be on my own during sad times. An article I'd read, said a million things on how living alone makes you a better person—hence the solo trip.

I boarded a local train from Malad to Churchgate. Being a Sunday, there was hardly any crowd. I sat at the window and started counting the stations going by. I was mourning over how people I loved so dearly went away without a trace. Many vendors had come into the compartment, selling everything from a needle to an aeroplane. I'm sure on weekdays even a ghost would be scared to enter this space. A voice stood out amidst the hullabaloo, 'Madam pen le lo, 10 rupaye ka ek,' urging me to buy a pen worth Rs 10. I raised my palm in refusal, without feeling the necessity of eye contact. She didn't persuade, she moved on, the voice became feeble.

Then after some time, I could hear the voice again. On an impulse I turned my head around. The woman selling pens was standing across me. I noticed that except her eyes, feet and hands, her whole body was covered. Burnt skin peeped through the light green chunni with which she had wrapped her head and face. I couldn't stop myself from sitting her down and asking her about the burns. Her answer did not surprise me—I figured she was an acid attack survivor by the look of her skin but I wanted her to confirm. She said yes, she was a survivor. I requested her to uncover her face and to my surprise, she didn't hesitate. I would lie if I said it didn't hurt. It hurt me more than anything else in the world to pretend to have a normal conversation with a human being whose only intact part was her voice.

I put up the bravest face to continue the conversation. My obvious questions didn't bother her and she began telling me about herself. I learnt that her boyfriend had poured a bottle of acid on her face and body when she refused to marry him. And her refusal was her family's decision—it wasn't hers. She bore the brunt of hurting a man's ego.

I tried hard not to notice the intensity of the scars on her feet and hands, but couldn't. My eyes kept falling on her feet every now and then as we were talking. When I asked her about what action her family took against the man, her voice grew strong as she said, *'Wo jail main hai',* he's behind bars. I must say it felt like the only satisfying thing I had heard in a long time about the law and order system around us.

Once she finished with her story, I looked up firmly and took her hands in mine. I comforted her and asked her what I could do to make her life easier. What would a surgery cost? I wasn't expecting this but she revealed the most bitter truth to me—that face was after surgery. It wasn't recoverable any further. Her disturbing statement had torn me to pieces but I did not lose my composure. I took her number, gave her mine and I let her go. I promised her that I would call. Till she remained in front of my eyes, I behaved like a strong-willed lady who had just counselled an acid attack survivor. Women watching had no idea how many internal tears I had shed. A couple of women sitting around applauded my effort but I just couldn't tell them how scarred and burnt I felt. A woman who could have been just as beautiful as I am has no reason to look into the mirror for the rest of her life!

How would she live through all these years? She would never have a career—no one hires a burnt face. Forget having a sex life, she would never endure a man's touch, would she? After all this? One of the worst things that can happen to a woman is being pushed into the flesh trade; this woman didn't qualify for that job either. Hundreds of questions rose and died within me till I reached the last station. I didn't get down, I returned in the same train. I kept sitting there, physically rooted but so moved emotionally that upon closing my eyes even for a second, her face would flash in my mind's eye. I didn't cry, I couldn't cry. I wanted to but my tears froze.

I hated myself for hating my life. I hated how I was cursing my loneliness. I hated the fact that people like me do not value what we have, where we are, our lives, our people, our situations, our comforts, and our abilities. A girl younger than me, nowhere close to my education, knowledge, career was making ends meet with absolutely no complaints. She didn't curse God even once. She didn't blame the society, neither did she blame her parents. But if I look at myself and the world around, the more we excel in our lives, the further we move away from contentment. We keep groaning over things that didn't happen to us. Would we survive if we had the experience Kavita underwent?

We are cowards, especially the corporate slaves who try to escape office on the weekdays and the household on weekends. We have no right to find faults in the system. We send less than ten mails in a day, sitting in AC offices, blogging about where this country is heading, retweeting a minister's statement, and posting pictures of expensive lunches with colleagues on Facebook. We need to step out into the real world and meet real people.

I did call Kavita. I have established a connect between her and an NGO. I will do whatever I can to help her find a job if not a face ('If that's what the Almighty wished,' Kavita says). I'm glad God made me meet her, it has changed me forever. That twenty-minute interaction will stay with me till my last breath. I cancelled my trip to Spain because I thought the same money could help her start a new life but she refused. She didn't want financial help, she wanted a job which she could pursue and give her life a new meaning. If I couldn't find her one, I would generate one for her. That's a promise I gave to her and to myself.

# New Year and Daddy

## HEERA NAWAZ

Last year, on New Year's Eve, while most of the world's population of men and women were stepping into their dancing shoes to dance their way into the coming year with words from songs like J. Lo's 'Waiting for tonight' quivering on their lips, I had to be different. Yes, on New Year's Eve, last year, I curled up on the couch in front of the TV (being the habitual couch potato that I am) and watched *Kabhi Khushi, Kabhi Gham*. Karan Johar, the master who has created many cinematic masterpieces (including *Kal Ho Naa Ho*), couldn't have evoked a more tear-jerking response with K3G, which he summed up in the simple yet telling words, 'It's all about loving your parents'.

Can a person ever get over a parent's death, that too, on a New Year's Eve? Well, exactly five years ago, I'd lost my father on this day. Since then, each New Year brings back cruel flashbacks of the time when I bade him a final adieu.

On that dark December night, when firecrackers were being burst to herald in the New Year, the velvety blackness of the sky sparkled with shiny stars, glittering like scintillating diamonds. Yet, these cold stars and diamonds lacked the warmth and genuineness of his very own Tara and Heera (my sister and I) as we watched Daddy slowly slip into unconsciousness.

Daddy had, from the time I was very small, always inspired me to keep New Year resolutions. 'Daddy, this year, I want to become beautiful and famous, like Princess Diana!' I exclaimed when I was a thirteen-year-old. At that age, one only sees the glamour, the sensation, and the extensive fan following of those who are famous without realizing that fame had a flip side, too—lack of privacy and normalcy. If I had known that stories of fairytale princesses do not always have fairytale endings, and that Diana herself used to loathe the constant flashes of the paparazzis' camera bulbs and their intrusion into her private life, I may have thought differently. But all that hadn't crossed my thirteen-year-old impressionable mind.

Our family had just shifted from Big Apple. And since New York City conditions people to be tough, we kids had wanted the New Year gifts to be materialistic and classy. I was especially glad that I had received three gifts, which had all been fastidiously wrapped in colourful paper.

'Daddy, my best gift is this stunning necklace!' I said, and I then showed the necklace, which had red and white stones embedded in a gaudy gold base, to him. As my father picked it up, out slipped another gift from another good friend. It was a placard, which had the words, 'A TRUE FRIEND—A FOUND TREASURE' engraved on it and below it was the name of my best friend, Poovamma.

My father then said the words, which I remember clearly, 'I know you are in a growing up phase along with the fact that having just come from America, materialistic gifts appear more valuable. However, the necklace reflects artificiality. But look at Poovamma's placard—it has a wealth of meaning in so few words! It is simple, telling and deep. Moreover, it is symbolic of true and reciprocal friendship, which is a gift of a lifetime. Your resolution for this year should not be to attain transient beauty and fame, but instead to have genuine friends like Poovamma.'

I thought back about how true my father's words were! Many of the gifts I have received on New Year over the years have faded into oblivion, but some of my most important friendships have stood the test of time. True friendship is something so precious and if earnest, it is something that not even rivals can take away. It is a resolution worth making, year after year.

I fumbled through my teens, making and breaking resolutions until I came to a New Year when I was nineteen years old. For a young woman on the threshold of life, nineteen is a dangerous age, for it is when one is physically a woman, but emotionally a confused girl searching for an identity— bewildered by boyfriends and career options.

That New Year I was with my father and I told him, 'Daddy, I've got so many New Year resolutions this year, it being the last New Year when I am a teenager. Can I tell you just four of my resolutions?'

'Sure,' said my father, 'Only see to it that they are not like building beautiful grey castles in the air.'

I sallied forth on my New Year resolutions. 'First of all, I plan to learn cooking, especially chocolate brownies and scrumptious pound cakes. Secondly, a talent I have always envied is an emotional singing voice, so I would like to learn singing. Thirdly, I also want to learn to play a musical instrument, preferably a piano or a guitar, and if possible, I may even start a pop group. How does "Cocktail Comrades" sound?' I saw my father cock up one eyebrow and look at me quizzically. 'No, Daddy, that's not all. My fourth resolution is to take lessons on public speaking to improve communication. I really hope these resolutions last in the New Year for, if not, I won't be a prim and proper lady. I'll just be myself,' I moaned.

My father's reaction was electric. 'There's absolutely no harm in being yourself! In fact, that could be your best New Year resolution—to grow in the place where you are planted. Never, ever be a contrived person. Be yourself. Pretty teenage girls like you can attract boys, like a magnet attracting nails. If you just remember to be yourself, you would find stable friendships.' My father's words held a vital message, which cut me to the quick.

After a rather emotional but telling adolescent phase, I reached the shores of adulthood, my New Year resolutions no longer reflecting the need for an identity, but instead centred on my new adult passion, which was writing. I had been bitten by the journalistic bug, and had begun writing reams on raindrops on roses and whiskers on kittens and everything else that took my fancy.

In fact, writing had become something of an obsession with me. I wrote like a person driven by imagination. I remained in my own cocoon of a world of writing, editing and proofreading, while I chiselled sentences like a sculptor and moulded them to capture the finer nuances of meaning. Needless to say, my college studies floundered, and I had to change to Arts in order to afford more time to write my poems, songs and short stories.

Unfortunately, while writing, I fell into a trap, which is decidedly dangerous—I began seeing things from the market's perspective, that sensational writing sells. So, I began writing gossipy items. Then on one New Year when I was twenty-one, I wrote a morbidly sensational article on the former diva, Marilyn Monroe, which was graphic and explicit in its description of her extramarital affairs.

My father was at his dentist's clinic where he happened to read this article. He got the shock of his life on seeing my name as the article's author. Broaching the topic to me would be delicate for I had not been open about it. He did not make direct reference to the article although he told me tactfully that I should make a number of resolutions regarding my writing. His exact words were, 'Avoid bombastic language and instead be simple in your writings. Write to express and not to impress. Don't misuse your talents, and however great the temptation, never resort to yellow journalism.'

Not once did he mention the article on that blonde bombshell. I felt deeply ashamed. What touched me the most was the way my father had handled the situation, cautiously, carefully, measuring each word without discouraging me and making me lose heart altogether. So, instead of dumping my obsession with writing, I, due to my father's tact, decided not to be stubbed out but to rise from the ashes like a Phoenix. My New Year resolution for that year was to write constructively as I enrolled in a 'Developmental Journalism' course.

As the years went by, my writing became more intense and diversified and I felt I needed a computer to facilitate editing. So, in the year 1997, my father bought a computer. Since only one person can use the computer at a time, we made a routine where both of us could use it in turns.

One morning, my father asked me to type out something for him. I flew off the handle and shouted, 'Look, in the morning, the computer is reserved for me!' My selfishness, which had been my major flaw, had taken an upper hand. I quickly shut down the computer and rushed for work. If only

I had looked back, I would have stopped in my tracks, for on my father's face, reflected a very hurt and grave expression.

To digress a bit, the year 1997 was the year when my father's health started deteriorating. As he was growing old, his nervous system had weakened. Yet, he was determined to complete writing his book, and he worked on it with steely grit and determination.

To get back to that particular day, the ugly and impulsive words that were spoken could not be taken back. After two hours of working in my office, HealthScribe (India) Limited, I suddenly got a telephone call from home. My mother told me that my father had taken seriously ill; she had admitted him to St John's Medical Hospital where she learnt that he needed to have an emergency treatment. Then my mother told me that even in that condition he had said that he wanted to talk to me.

I could feel tears flowing as if they would never stop. I took the office car to St John's Medical Hospital, and saw my father's weakened frame on a stretcher. After a few hours when the treatment was over and the effect of anaesthesia had worn off, I took my father on the stretcher trolley back to the hospital room.

In his weak condition, he told me, 'I'm sorry about today. I should have understood.'

I burst into a flood of uncontrollable tears and cried, 'No Daddy, I'm sorry. I should have understood.' I held his hand and cried my heart out. 'Daddy,' I cried, 'My resolution for this year is to strive to become selfless and more sensitive to family members, to become helpful and to live for others.'

My father had to stay on in the hospital because he had become too weak and he needed constant supervision. The year 1997 passed. As the months of the year 1998 went by, my father's health deteriorated. Then came the day, 31 December 1998. It was two in the morning when in the hospital, my father suddenly woke up and started vomiting thick red blood. It came to him as a shock. He cried out, 'I want to see my children . . .' But it was 2 a.m. and my mother did not want us to come to the hospital in those wee hours. As soon as dawn broke, however, we rushed to the hospital. I hugged my father who had been 'my friend, philosopher and guide' and who had taught me over all the years the difference between right and wrong.

In a feeble voice, he said, 'Lead a life that will make me proud of you. Continue your writing and touch hearts the way you have touched mine.'

I burst into tears and whispered to him, 'You've been the best father a girl could have. You have given me the best education, the best life. I'm just another part of you.'

Then, suddenly, blood began oozing from his mouth at an almost frightening rate. In tears, I alerted the nurse and quickly we had to move to another room in the hospital to find out whether the bleeding could be stopped. Outside this room, he motioned to me that he wanted to write something. I whispered to him, 'Daddy, don't strain yourself.' Yet, he persisted. So, I got him a paper and pencil on which he struggled to write, 'Dr Vinod, Happy New Year.' I later came to know that my father knew that Dr Vinod was a physically handicapped doctor who was very kind and considerate.

After the treatment, we took my father back to his room. All along the huge corridors of the hospital were beautiful Christmas decorations, kaleidoscopic bulbs, colourful streamers, and models of Jesus Christ. All the decorations reminded me of the Christmases and New Years over the past years which I had celebrated with my father. I thought about all the New

Year resolutions I had made and the learnings my father had imbibed in me, and how wonderfully he had moulded me from being a carefree, selfish and impulsive young girl to a thoughtful and deep woman.

But time was running out. At exactly 10.30 p.m. on New Year's Eve, my father died. I cried uncontrollably as the only man who ever meant anything to me was now gone. I felt the best way of paying tribute to my father who had always wanted me to lead an ethical, God-fearing life was to the make the following words of Stephen Grellet my New Year resolution:

*'I expect to pass through this world but once. Any good thing I can do, therefore, or any kindness I can show to any fellow creature, let me do it now. Let me not defer or neglect it, for I shall not pass this way again.'*

# *Unforgiven*

### SNIGDHA KHATAWKAR MAHENDRA

Everyone knew how much Rathin Mitra and his wife had suffered because of Samir, their eldest son-in-law. Chaoni, Rathin's eldest daughter, had not visited her parents' house ever since her marriage to Samir. Samir would not allow her to go to her parents' house threatening that if she ever visited them, she should never return. The Mitras had not seen their eldest daughter in almost thirty years. A year back, Rathin's wife had suddenly taken ill at night. All through the night she kept telling Rathin to speak to Samir and get Chaoni back. It remained the lady's last wish for she passed away by dawn.

In the days that followed, Rathin called up Samir many times but could not get either him or Chaoni on the phone. Rathin also wrote a letter explaining the recent developments but received no reply. A year passed and now Rathin was on his deathbed. He knew it and so did the others around him.

Yet, he was not willing to die. He wanted to see Samir and Chaoni. He kept calling out their names.

As time passed, Rathin's desire to meet his son-in-law and daughter reached a feverish pitch. He kept begging everyone to call them. His four other sons-in-law who had only heard of this awful brother-in-law were getting irritated. They had been model sons-in-law till then, but the old man was not even asking about them. Their wives, who barely knew their sister for they were pretty young when Chaoni was married off, were equally angry. Chaoni was married at nineteen, her sisters had been eleven, nine, six and four then. All their lives they had only heard ill things about their brother-in-law and so each one had groomed their husbands in a manner that would make them appear good in the eyes of their parents. Each wanted her father to recognize her husband as the best.

Chaoni, being Rathin's first daughter, held a special place in his heart. That she was also a beautiful baby made her all the more dear to her father. Even after she grew up Rathin would always remember her as the sweet, chubby, beatific baby. Both he and his wife had wanted nothing but the best for Chaoni. They had thought that Samir would be the perfect groom with whom their daughter would lead a happy married life. Samir had all the qualities that a girl's family looks for. He was good-looking, friendly, well-educated, well-settled, and hailed from a good family. The only concern had been that he was an only child whose father had passed away when he was very young.

Relatives kept suggesting to Rathin that the mother might be too possessive of her son, which might make Chaoni's life difficult but Samir's mother appeared very kind and Rathin fixed the marriage. In those days of arranged marriages, the bride was usually not allowed to meet or speak to the groom alone before marriage so Chaoni and Samir never spoke to each other. Had Rathindranath permitted that, the story of this marriage would have been very different.

Things started to go wrong immediately after the wedding. It was customary for the bride to be accompanied by someone from her own house who would stay with her for a few days to make the transition into the new surroundings easier. Chaoni's younger sister, Lekha, had travelled with Chaoni to Allahabad. Lekha was eight years younger than Chaoni. She had not understood much but had told her mother that the groom and bride did not share a bedroom. Samir had refused to sleep in the same room as her sister. He had also asked his mother to arrange for Lekha's departure soon. Samir and Chaoni were expected to drop Lekha back at Jabalpur but Samir flatly refused to do so. He was okay to let Chaoni go. Rathin understood that it was a ploy to get rid of Chaoni. So he arranged for his second daughter to be picked up by a friend who had gone for a dip in the Sangam.

In those days parents did not interfere in a married girl's life. After her marriage, a woman was expected to have minimum ties with her parental home. Likewise, Rathin and his wife stayed away from Chaoni's life. They did not hear from her. They would write to her but never received any letter from her. They hoped and prayed that Chaoni was fine. Some years later, Lekha's marriage got fixed. Rathin went to invite Chaoni and family for the marriage. When he reached Samir's house, Samir refused to meet him but Rathin met Chaoni. Chaoni was still the same. Everyone had told him that she would change after her marriage but Rathin could see that this was not the case with his daughter. Nothing about her had changed.

Her eyes had lit up when she had seen him. She had hugged him and asked him about her mother and her sisters. She had

also wept and said she missed them a lot. Rathin had wanted
to bring her home right away but a father of five daughters
does not take such a risk. So he had left Chaoni in her marital
house though Samir's mother asked him to not leave without
his daughter. Chaoni did not come for her younger sister's
wedding. A few days later Rathin telephoned Chaoni. From
her they got to know that Samir's mother had passed away,
a few weeks before Lekha's wedding. Immediately after her
death, Samir had got a new woman in the house, a nurse by
profession. In spite of all this, on his death bed, Rathin kept
asking for Samir.

Samir saw no point in visiting his father-in-law. Chaoni
was not interested in her parents any more, she was happier
with Samir. Immediately after her marriage she had cried for
her family day and night but after thirty years, Samir's house
had become her home and she never spoke about her father or
mother, unless, they telephoned to speak to her. Even then she
referred to 'Baba' and 'Ma' as if they were mere names. No, he
would not go, he thought. However, Rathin's thought kept
coming to his mind. The old man wanted to see his daughter
one last time, was he doing the right thing by denying him
that? He remembered reading a letter from Rathin that he had
received after coming back from a two-month long holiday.
It had mentioned his wife's death and her dying wish to see
Chaoni and him. In the letter Rathin had requested them to
come and visit. Samir had rejected the idea. Chaoni's parents
had abandoned her by marrying her to him. Why did they
want to meet her now? Did they want to apologize and cleanse
their souls before dying?

He was not interested in helping them attain their peace.
Samir had suffered a lot because of the Mitras. Long back he
had decided that he would never forgive them but the tide of

time is more powerful than a mere human's desire to leave things unchanged, and Samir was a mere human. Rathin and his wife kept playing on his mind till Samir gave in. After all he was a kind man. He and Chaoni left for Jabalpur to meet Rathin the same evening.

All through the journey, the past flashed before Samir's eyes. Thirty years back he had returned with Chaoni on a similar train. Of course there was no second AC then, the *baraat* had travelled first class. He had not let Rathin pay for the baraat's tickets. He was totally against such practices. The family business was doing well; he had money, then, why trouble the father of five daughters with this additional burden? How happy and eager he had been to get married. His heart was buzzing and so was his stomach. For four months, ever since the marriage had been fixed, he had carried Chaoni's picture in his pocket. At night, he would dream about how life after marriage would be. Friends had teased him saying that he had not stopped smiling since his marriage had been fixed. Some also complained that many girls had become despondent after hearing the announcement of his marriage. To such comments Samir had laughed jollily. He was not a proud fellow but knew that he was considered handsome; and then Chaoni was also pretty. With her almond-shaped, hazel-coloured eyes, curly jet-black hair, heart-shaped face, porcelain skin and pink lips she had made herself a place in his heart. If ever there was a child-woman face, it was her. She had looked so beautiful in the wedding sari! He had never been as happy as he had been on his wedding day.

However, he had felt something was amiss once during the wedding ceremony. There was no particular incident but it was the look that Chaoni had in her eyes when she looked at him during the *shubho drishti*. When it was time for the *bidaai*, Chaoni was all tears and no cajoling from anyone worked.

Somehow they managed to get her into the car and leave. Her parents did not come to drop her off at the station. Throughout the journey, Chaoni stayed quiet. Samir only caught glimpses of her as she remained firmly attached to her sister and refused to come and sit next to Samir. He did not mind that. It was during the *ful shoja* that he got to know the truth. Chaoni bit him when he tried to get close to her. He apologized profusely and tried to talk to her. It was then that he realized that this girl of nineteen had the brain development of a seven-year-old. That entire night Samir sat in the balcony of his room. His mind felt dead. He could not comprehend why Rathin Mitra had played this cruel joke on him.

Samir called off the wedding reception. He did not want to make a fool of himself. Annoyed at the deception, his mother called up Rathin to demand an explanation. To all her accusations, Rathin kept giving the time-tested answers used by all fathers who do not want to trouble themselves over their daughters. Samir's mother felt like turning Chaoni out of the house right then but could not. *Where could she send this girl with the intelligence of a seven-year-old but beauty of a nineteen-year-old?* She was not as inhuman as Chaoni's parents had been!

After Chaoni's sister left, Chaoni became completely uncommunicative and fell ill. Samir's mother nurtured her back to health. After that Chaoni attached herself to her mother-in-law. She would follow her around like a pet wherever she went and did small chores for her. In the initial years, Samir's mother took care of Chaoni. She knew she had groomed her son well so he would never hurt Chaoni but she wondered what would happen of him. After giving it some thought, Samir's mother contacted a lawyer to get Samir divorced. She planned to get Samir free of the entanglement and yet let Chaoni stay with them. Samir, however, did not agree to the divorce. She pestered him day and night over it but Samir just did not agree. He could not explain to his mother. If there was such a thing as love, he had experienced it. He had fallen in love with that image of Chaoni, and no one could take that place.

After many years Chaoni was very happy when her father came to visit her. Seeing her so happy, Samir's mother begged Rathin to take her back but Rathin did not. Samir's mother was getting old. She worried about both Samir and Chaoni. *Who would take care of them should something happen to her?* Then, all of a sudden she passed away. She was alone at home with Chaoni when she had a heart attack. Chaoni saw that her new mother was not moving. She nudged and nudged her but the lady did not get up—that is how the neighbours and Samir found them. Chaoni, once again, became the sad, lonely child that she had been when she first came to the house. She missed Samir's mother. Samir could not take care of her but could not leave her alone either. He hired a nurse to take care of her in his absence.

In the thirty years, many-a-times Samir yearned for another woman, many-a-times he found himself drawn to other women, many-a-times he felt like pushing Chaoni out of his life but he did not do any of those things. After his mother passed away, he found it difficult to balance the demands of a growing business with the demands of having a hapless wife at home so he sold his business and took up a job where he had to serve regular hours. From a rich businessman he started living the life of an ordinary middle-class man and did not complain. The only people Samir hated for many years were the Mitras. He just could not understand why they did what they did! They had not only deceived him but were also being extremely cruel to their own daughter. *How could they allow their child to undergo mental and physical abuse?* He felt nothing but disgust and revulsion towards them. As time passed he gradually got over his anger for them too, but was so disconnected from the whole thing that he felt that he had no responsibility towards them.

In defence of the Mitras, the only thing that can be said was that they had five daughters to be married off. If the eldest daughter was not married there would have been problems marrying off the other four. If the eldest daughter was mentally challenged, it would be assumed that all the daughters had the same problem.

All their well-wishers had told them that girls like Chaoni recovered after marriage. Marriage, meaning sex, was supposed to cure any ailment in any unmarried Indian's personality. It did not work in Chaoni's case because Samir refused to sleep with her.

When Samir broke off all ties with the Mitras it gave them complete freedom. Samir was painted as the evil son-in-law and they became the helpless parents of a tortured girl. Chaoni's sisters were much younger to her and remembered little. A lie repeated over and over again becomes the truth and so even the people who knew how Chaoni was, slowly forgot it.

Rathin, on his death bed, could not forget how he and his wife had mauled the honesty and kindness of a mother and her son, and wanted nothing more but to apologize to him. He knew that he may not be forgiven for having ruined the man's life but he wanted to try. In his delirium he tried to tell the truth to those around him but they did not comprehend. It was only after his death when Samir reached there with Chaoni that the truth was suddenly clear to all. It was Rathin's fate to die without seeing his daughter, to die not knowing whether he was forgiven or not.

# Bigger than a Bee Sting

BISWAS (BUDDH) TIMSHINA

**YEAR 2011**

'You promised!' Since force wasn't a feasible option to use on her six-feet-tall son, she used emotional blackmail.

'I know, I promised. That's why I'm trying to open my eyes.' My eyes had been glued shut by my own reluctance to open them at six in the morning. The last time I had seen Gangtok at six in the morning had been when I had to wake up to pee.

Laboriously, I opened my eyes, to find Ama ready with the camera in her hand and fully clad in *gunyo–chollo*—a typical Nepali dress worn during festivities or ceremonies. The hair was neatly done and there was a slight hint of make-up on her skin. The lipstick was bright and so was the *potay*, the Nepali necklace worn by married women. Her appearance could put a sixteen-year-old to shame.

I put on a T-shirt and dragged my feet sleepily, all the way to the terrace. Baba was there, watering his plants, the plants he loved more than his son.

'The plants never ask for an expensive phone, all they need is water,' he would say.

Ama animatedly walked around the terrace, trying to find a spot for the photoshoot. I told her to stand by the pine saplings. The next major concern was to get the right pose. She tried a pose, placing her index finger on the cheek. 'Ama, you are forty-five, not sixteen!' I said.

'*Dil toh chota hai na,*' she misquoted—the heart is always a kid. I corrected her but she wasn't really paying attention. She was busy trying out different poses. Baba simply smiled at his wife's unwillingness to act her age.

'Okay. Ready?' we finally narrowed it down to a few poses and I captured them. The honking of the horn put an end to our photo session.

'Oh! I am late!' she exclaimed and ran downstairs to the road where a Bolero awaited her.

'Aren't you going?' I asked Baba, who had gotten back to admiring his plants, now that his wife had left.

He gave me that look which said *he didn't want to but he had to*, 'Programme starts at ten,' he said with so much disinterest that I felt sorry for him.

This programme was a big deal for Ama. We all knew what it meant to her but one couldn't completely dislodge the fact that it was a boring affair. The unveiling of the new cultural music video album was to take place in the Tadong College Auditorium, by a renowned minister. The launch of the album was to be followed by a long and tedious speech by the chief guest, concerning the need to preserve our culture while he played with the buttons of his new Gucci blazer.

Then, over-aged women, including Ama, would dance to the tunes of the songs from the album. This was going to be followed by *Bhagavad Gita* recitals by school children. The programme would end after a few more speeches from people who liked to speak. Not a programme that would excite my father.

All this was being done by the Nepali Sanskritik Sangrakshan Samiti, a committee that aimed at preserving Nepali culture in this over-anglicized world. It was formed majorly by the women of Fifth Mile and Sixth Mile, Tadong, Gangtok, Sikkim. Ama held the position of the treasurer in the committee, which required that she reach the venue four hours before the programme started.

The day passed by without much activity. I was enjoying my vacation reading new books, while my sister Anu was enjoying a whole day of slumber. The only time she woke up was to make lunch for Baba before he left for the programme, after which she went back to her cosy bed. I wondered where she got all that sleepiness from. Maybe she slept so much that she got tired of sleeping, which led to her sleep more. Realizing how stupid that thought was, I started going through the pictures that I had taken that morning.

I had seen my mother's youthful pictures from the past (in sepia) and everything had changed since. She had gained weight, her hair had become short and she didn't wear skirts any more. One thing however, seemed to have been plastered on her since birth—her smile. The long wide curve on her face, that she always liked to show off, hadn't reduced a millimetre over the past few years.

Not even during the darkest days of her life, did she lose that smile.

～

YEAR 2009

'Listen, listen,' Ama said. She had asked me to keep my ears close to her knees while she straightened one. A click sound escaped from her right knee and she laughed, as if noises escaping from joints were a humorous affair. She bent the leg to another click. Again she laughed.

'Ama, dinner is ready!' Anu brought her food in her small *jharkey thaal*, brass plate. She tried to stand up to get to the wash basin but couldn't, so I helped her. With difficulty she took a few steps, which made me make her sit down again. I brought her some water in a jug so that she would wash her hands without having to walk.

'Feels like I am a queen!' she said, enjoying the extra hospitality. I looked at Baba who smiled half-heartedly, he was worried about his wife's health.

The doctors from Gangtok and Siliguri were stalling us with weird theories about Ama's leg. Then Baba, out of nowhere, decided to take her some place else.

'Where?' I asked him.

'Anywhere but here,' he said and the next day booked a flight to Delhi.

Once in Delhi, Baba and Ama would call us once a day. They talked about the doctor they met and the various tests that were performed on her. 'You know, the doctor continuously asked me about my pink cheeks. He even asked me to test my blood for hemo . . . hemolobin.'

'Haemoglobin,' I corrected her. 'And it sounds like the doctor was flirting with you,' I added.

'He looks like your grandfather.'

'So if he looked younger, you wouldn't mind?'

'No,' she whispered through the phone. It took some time for our laughter to settle down.

~

'The doctor says that its arthritis,' Anu told me once I was back from school.

'What is arthritis? How bad is it?' I asked her. She didn't know so I called Baba immediately.

'What is it?' I asked with a racing heart.

'It's just rheumatoid arthritis.' Baba said, as if Ama was diagnosed with fever, and a few pills would cure her. My heart calmed down.

'The doctor has to take out some fluid from her joints, so it might take a few more days.' He was at his reassuring best.

~

The neighbours often asked me about my mother and I would casually tell them that it was just arthritis. No one knew what it was but from my nonchalant attitude they thought it to be something minor, like a bee sting. No one knew about the danger it possessed, and that it could cripple a person for life. Even I didn't know.

It was the Internet that enlightened me.

The webpage displayed an image of a hand affected by rheumatoid arthritis. My heart sank. The skin in the image had turned dark and the fingers were anything but straight, like the hands of the ghosts in a low-budget Hindi horror movie. A bee-stung hand looked a lot better than this, I thought. It felt like a black hole had sucked the life out of my body as I went through the images, horrified.

'What are you doing?' Anu walked in and I hurriedly closed the window. My panic, as well as the wallpaper on display, might have made her think that I was watching porn, so she awkwardly walked out.

~

Baba and Ama returned within a week's time. Ama had to be supported as she walked up the stairs. I helped her to the living room and went to Baba who had gone to the terrace to smoke. 'Baba . . .' I bowed; he threw away the cigarette and blessed me with his hands.

'You told me about it like she had fever,' I scolded him. He shot me that fatherly glance and I controlled my voice. 'You should have told us the truth. We had the right to know how dangerous arthritis is,' I said, a little softer.

'How did you know?'

'The Internet.'

'Internet can tell you all that also?' Baba asked. He didn't know half of what the Internet could do. 'Did you tell Anu?' he asked.

'No,' I replied.

'Why?'

'She would be worried,' I answered. He didn't reply but just smiled.

~

Turns out that even Anu knew about the dangers of being diagnosed with arthritis from the start but she didn't want to blow the bubble that I lived in. A puzzling family ours is, I tell you.

~

'Aren't you scared? I asked Ama. We were sitting in the terrace under the warm winter sun, enjoying oranges freshly picked and delivered from our village, Lingmoo. She wasn't allowed citrus fruits but I gave her one, promising that I wouldn't tell Baba. As she removed the skin off the orange, she nodded. She was scared. Even though she didn't show it, she was scared.

She wasn't a woman who would sit all day long watching brainwashing serials on the idiot box. She liked working, going places and dancing in her heels. She wasn't sure if she could do that again in the future. She was scared but she never let it show. She was, always, her true smiling self.

The doctor had asked Ama to return for a review after three months. He was amazed to see the improvement and mentioned that he had never seen such a fast recovery. Baba said all this over the phone. I, however, had my doubts. 'This time I'm telling the truth,' he said. Maybe he was, for he sounded truly happy. 'But I don't know why the doctor keeps talking about her pink cheeks.' I could smell his jealousy even over the phone. 'Baba, the doctor is my grandfather's age,' I said.

~

'No. I am not selling the shop!' She put a full stop to the whole argument and walked down to open her shop.

Ama owned a gift shop on the ground floor of our building and it had been functioning since I was in Class II. It had become a part of Ama's existence and it was hard to imagine Ama's life without the gift shop. But the shop was three floors down and the doctor had strictly asked her to avoid staircases. The shop had been closed while she was bedridden but since she could now walk, she wanted to open it again. We tried to persuade her to give up the shop but she wouldn't listen. 'It's just arthritis, I am not dead,' she said.

Balancing her body with the help of the railing, she would walk down to her shop every morning, ready to make some money, and return home only after seven in the evening. People often came to our house with their 'Get Well Soon' goodies to see the arthritis patient but ended up buying a dinner set or a cosmetic item from the patient's gift shop.

~

YEAR 2011

The creaking of the door startled me and the camera nearly fell off my hands. I turned around to find Ama peeking through the door, her hair a mess. Sweat beads had formed a transparent moustache above her lips, indicating that there had been a lot of dancing after the programme had ended. 'Come,' she said and signalled with her hand, which held a freshly wrapped DVD.

Baba directly went to bed, probably due to all the sleep that had accumulated during the course of the programme. Anu, Ama and I sat in the living room with the laptop in front of us. I clicked the play button and the image of the Saraswati-Dolma Mandir in Fifth Mile, Tadong. The video started off with the following words:

'Nepali Sanskritik Sangrakshan Samiti presents . . .'

Ama clapped as the first song of the album played. It was shot in Lekship Mandir, near Jorethang and started off with a pretty lady in a red saree dancing to the tune of a flute. As the song went on, hundreds of forty-plus women danced in the backdrop with their hands folded in devotion to the lord.

'There I am,' Ama pointed at the screen.

'Where . . . where?' I asked.

'It went,' she said slowly.

'Oh there . . . there,' she said after a few seconds.

This time I paused the video and searched for Ama in the crowd. She was at a corner of the frame with her hands paused in the air and mouth open.

'Wooooooooo . . .' Anu and I cheered her and Ama turned pinker than her normal self. 'Our Ama is in a music video.'

I poked her in the stomach and she gave a shy laugh. 'Stop it,' she said, hitting me on the arms.

'There . . .', 'There . . .', '. . . and there . . .' she pointed out every time she appeared on the screen. I wasn't enjoying the video as much as I was enjoying her enjoying the video.

Just two years ago she needed to think twice before going to the bathroom and here she was dancing like arthritis had never happened. The shoot wasn't easy for her. They had shot five songs in and around Gangtok, which meant dedicating more than a week to it. Dawn to dusk she would be in some location jumping around with her arthritic legs. Every night she would drag her body to her room, trying hard to hide the pain behind her smile, and fall asleep to wake up next morning and walk back to the shoot site like she had replaced her old legs with ones.

The DVD was a compilation of her spirit and ardour and she enjoyed every frame of it with her trademark smile accompanied by her tearful eyes. It was only when my sight turned blurry that I realized my eyes were watery as well.

~

PRESENT

She has given away the shop. Not because she can't handle it but because she has a crusher plant to look after. Yes, she drives herself every day to Tanak with those arthritic legs and ensures that boulders are crushed into pebbles smoothly in the plant. And she is still dancing around in different programmes organized by the Nepali Sanskritik Sangrakshan Samiti. She misses wearing heels, though she did find that dancing in flats is easier.

She may have been crippled physically, once in her life, but arthritis could never ever cripple her spirit. Of course, arthritis would not have been easy to conquer on her own but her better half, my father, helped a lot. He made sure that she got her daily dosage of medicines prescribed by the doctor and love prescribed by his heart. And that smile on my old lady's face is a reflection of the love that my old man has showered on her.

The doctors say that we should credit the speedy recovery to God. Keeping the doctors' words in mind, I sincerely thanked Baba and Ama for helping Ama recover sooner than expected. Well, my parents are my God.

She still has crackling sounds coming out from her joints. After all, one cannot simply erase arthritis from one's life. But Ama thinks nothing of it. I totally love it!

With her attitude towards life, the love that she shares with Baba and the wonderful smile on her face, all surrounding me, I don't need to go far for inspiration. Right now my inspiration is on the terrace having a cup of Darjeeling tea.

# Giving Up or Standing Tall

### RUPALI TIWARI

People love happy endings. But not every story has a happy ending. And such stories are mostly forgotten with the thought that sadness is a part of life. Happy stories give hope and sad stories show us the mirror.

She always believed in happy endings. That one day a knight in shining armour will come and save the day. She loved the stories of Snow White and Cinderella where evil was surpassed by good. She was a nice girl. Right from the start. From the day she was born. I won't say that she was an angel. But she wasn't the devil either. Everyone loved her as a child is loved. Or maybe more. Who knows? Her parents doted on her. She was born with a silver spoon. Not exactly. But yes. Her life wasn't difficult either. She was happy. And had every reason to be. Life isn't always a fairytale. But it isn't a bed of thorns either.

I have heard that she was a very chirpy child. Very happy and irritating sometimes. I was happy and excited to meet her.

I had heard so much about her right from her dimpled cheeks to her boisterous laughter, I was dying to meet her. I had heard she knew how to live life to the fullest.

She had lost her father at the age of fifteen and was left with her mother and a little sister and a huge swarm of relatives who didn't give a damn whether her family lived or not. Her mother was a respectable scientist and that was one point in her favour.

I was struck by the sparkle in her eyes and dimples when I first met her. I didn't know where to start from. I had just failed my 12th board. I was on the brink of depression and had attempted suicide once when my mother asked her for help.

She was ready at once.

Without any question or any formality, she smiled warmly at me as if I was a family member. She welcomed me in her home. I didn't know what she would do to make me see the better part of my life. It was a secret that I was going to kill myself once I was free from there.

She handed me a glass of water and sat opposite me on the chair. I looked around in her room where different sketches and posters were hanging from the wall. I could see a book shelf as tall as the wall filled with all types of books and novels. God! She was a voracious reader. I could see a study table filled with pictures of her and her sister and trophies from her college. A typical teenager's room. Though she wasn't a teenager. She was more an aunt at the age of twenty-three. Must be her sister's idea of room decoration, I thought. She doesn't seem that type of a person to me.

As long as it took me to survey her room, she was staring at me. Smiling. Weird. She shouldn't be doing that! It makes people uncomfortable. I fidgeted in my seat. She waited for me to start.

'Nice room,' I started. She sat there smiling.

'Thanks. I drew everything in here. And that is my personal collection,' she pointed to the book shelf.

'I see,' I nodded. Without seeing anything.

'Don't worry. I won't be lecturing you on anything, ' she said. 'I want you to tell me why you attempted suicide.'

I stared at her matter-of-factly. Is she really dumb or what? Didn't she know that my life was over! I have failed my boards. A student's life ends when he or she fails.

'I wanted to try something new!' I said sarcastically.

She laughed. That booming laughter. I just stared at her. She was dumb.

'Okay. All right. I won't stop you the next time you want to do something like this. But I want you to listen to a story.'

Story? I hated them.

'Look. I know you want to help me. But please don't. I don't want to hear your stories. I already know that your dad died when you were of my age. I know you have seen a lot more than me but hey, wake up! I lost my dad too. Don't you dare say that I shouldn't be disheartened.'

'I won't say anything like that.' Her voice was sad now. No smile on her face. 'I wasn't going to tell you anything about myself. I thought that a story like Cinderella's or Snow White's won't make you happy. I never thought of myself as a survivor, you know. I merely tried to live.' She had a distant expression on her face. 'What do you know about me ?' she asked turning towards me.

'I know that you were an average student and that your dad died when you were young. But you still achieved what you wanted. Life isn't as easy as yours is, you know. You were helped by your grandfather. Your grandfather paid for your tuition and settled you in this house. I don't have any godfather like that. No one is going to save me from this. No one will come and say that it's okay if you failed your boards. Everyone is going to blame me for this.' I was on the brink of losing myself again. I stopped and took a deep breath.

'I would say that it's okay that you failed your boards. That it's fine if you failed this one time. It's not everything you know,' she said, sympathy written on her face.

'I don't want your sympathy!' I shouted at her. 'I just want to die. My life isn't as easy as yours. You get that!'

'I hope that you never see what I have seen, dear,' she replied with a distant look on her face.

I didn't know what to say. We sat in silence for couple of minutes. Before I could break it, she started, 'My father wasn't as idealistic as you think.' She turned towards me. 'He cheated on my mom.'

I stared at her open-mouthed. 'He never loved my mother. My mom did not love him either. Life is a bitch. And then you die,' she said and turned towards the window. 'You think that my life is easy? Think again. The grandfather that you are praising, he tried to rape me after three months of my dad's death.'

I stared at her expressionless face, dumbstruck.

'Do you know what it feels like when a person whom you trusted . . . who has seen you grow up . . . who has seen you in your diapers places his hands on your chest ? When the same person who has given you piggyback rides when you were a toddler starts fondling your breasts pretending innocence? When the same person tries to touch your naked back by pulling up your T-shirt? When the same person touches you in the most private way and all you can do is stare at him. Dumbstruck?'

She said all this with an expressionless face. She wasn't present there mentally.

'How did you . . . ?' I couldn't complete the question. Didn't know what to ask. What do you ask a girl who has seen all this? What do you ask her? Whether he succeeded or not?

'No, he didn't succeed. I locked myself in my room pretending to change my dress and didn't come out till my mom returned. I told her everything and that was the last time I was ever left alone with him.' She turned towards me with a serene smile.

'You didn't do anything ? I mean like put him behind bars?' I asked.

'What do you do when you have a sister to think of and a mother who is supported by her father? When that same father tries to rape you? You just stay shut. Because you have to think about everyone. No, I didn't do anything. I kept shut,' she said with that same smile

'How can you still smile? With everything that has happened . . . how could you leave everything behind and move on ?'

'That is what you need to learn, my dear. Things happen. Some terrible and some mild. But you have to know what are your priorities. Whether you let these things push you down or whether you look at your loved ones and decide to stand up again.' She looked into my eyes. 'I decided to think about my family. About their happiness. And I knew my problems were minor, as large was their happiness for me. Always have someone whose happiness matters more to you than your own. Everyone says your happiness is the most important, . . . but your happiness may fail you sometimes. If someone else's happiness is more important to you then you will be happy just to see that person smile.'

'How can you say all this with that smile ?' I was confused. How can she still be so normal?

'My family smiles when I smile. So do I. It's all in the circle. You are happy for the person you love and that person is happy to see you happy. Life doesn't always serve you on a silver platter. Sometimes you have to search for it.'

'Do you still see him ?' I asked, sympathetically.

'Yes. I do. He comes home often. And places his hand on my head. Though I duck out of his touch. But still. I do see him. And it's mandatory for me. I can't make my mother lose her father as I did mine. I want to see her happy. That's all.' Saying that she flashed a full dimpled smile.

I did not know what she has seen or not. Or whether she was right or wrong.

My mom came to take me back. By the time I was in the car, she was smiling again. That same full dimpled smile. She winked at me once and then waved me off.

I didn't know whether I was a better human or not after this encounter. But I knew this much, that I could survive this.

'I want to join school again, Ma. I will reappear in the exams,' I told my mother. She gave a startled cry and thanked God for this.

Somewhere she was right. I was happy seeing my mother smile because of me. She did know some things if not everything. I don't worship her nor is she my ideal but I am not going to kill myself for now.

I know she coped with the downs of life. And so can I.

# A Love So Unconditional

### RICHA TALUKDAR

It was that time of year when hospitals were the counterpart of our home. My father was operated for gall bladder stones and so he had to visit the hospital for weekly check-ups for a couple of months on Sundays. As expected, the place would be teeming with people and the seats outside the doctor's cabin would be full of diversely ill patients waiting for their turns for hours and hours.

My father did not like to take me along with him as after waiting and standing there for hours, when our turn would finally come, only he was allowed to enter the cabin because of some specific tests that the doctor thought would be traumatizing for me. My father thought I would be bored and tired and that it was better I didn't go along. But each time I somehow managed by insisting. Though he was right on the tired part, I never found hospitals boring. I was strangely fascinated by a huge number of things there and mostly by the different people, their families and the intense emotions in their eyes that one wouldn't see in such abundance elsewhere.

On one such Sunday, when I was in the hospital, loitering around, I saw that man again. He was probably one of the workers as he was wearing the hospital uniform but what attracted my attention was his strange behaviour. I often saw him peeping into a patient's room. Once or twice I even saw some senior authorities scolding him and asking him to work but that would not make him go away. He would stare into the room and smile to himself. The nurses mostly ignored his presence. The doctors, too, wouldn't react much. But his suspicious presence was bothering me a lot and I found it creepy. I couldn't just ignore and let it be.

I stood there for few minutes and after a while I finally thought of talking to him. I went up to him and asked if he knew the patient inside. He stared at me blankly and then ignored me. This made me more suspicious so I warned him I'd complain to the hospital management and authorities.

'I am Mahesh,' he said calmly and took me inside the room. 'Look, you woke her up!'

I stood inside the room, confused. I was suspecting him of something wrong.

'How's Sree?' he asked the young patient.

She smiled at him and pointed towards the doll lying beside her and said, 'She is sleeping.'

Mahesh turned to me and said, 'She is Kashvi. She is suffering from cerebral palsy. She was mentally stable at birth but over the years due to the negligence of her parents, her condition has turned worse.'

I looked at her. Everything about her was so serene. The word 'innocent' would be too small to describe those eyes. And the way she was sitting—with blithe carefreeness. She was not even worried about her looks. The uncombed hair, chapped lips, dry skin, and flowing nose; nothing bothered her. The hospital gown was falling off her shoulder and I could see bruises all over her hands that were apparently caused by excessive injections.

I went near her and touched her hand. I touched those bruises and bumps. She then pushed my hand away and looked at me in anger. Maybe I had hurt her. I looked into Mahesh's eyes, unsure of what to say. I was sympathetic but mostly I felt uneasy. I had tears in my eyes.

'Four years ago her parents brought her here,' Mahesh said. 'When she first came, her condition was worse than ever. She wouldn't listen to anyone and wouldn't even eat. She would often get these attacks where she would scream, cry, and throw everything around and even tried to harm herself. It was very difficult to control her. One such time when things got out of hand and she started getting fits, the nurses just couldn't control her and called me for help. That was the first time I saw her.' Mahesh said that with a warm smile and deep affection in his eyes. 'I asked the nurse about Kashvi,' Mahesh continued, 'She told me that Kashvi's parents couldn't look after her any more. It was difficult for them to keep a watch on her every second. They do pay for her treatment and visit her but are too busy to be able to give her much care, which was very necessary. The nurse also told me about her eating habits. She won't even look at food for days until she is dying of hunger and when she finally ate, she would vomit out most of it.

'I then went near Kashvi with a bowl of soup. I raised a spoon but she instantly turned her face and when I tried a little more, she pushed me away. I knew forcing her would worsen the situation. All she needed was a little extra love, care and attention. I know that her parents do love her and are very much concerned, but they never showed it to her. Maybe they never thought that could help her heal.'

Mahesh went near Kashvi. She was falling asleep. He looked at her and started running his finger through her hair.

'The first time I saw her I could feel a pain in her cry, a glimpse of suffering in her screams; it tormented me. I barely knew her but whenever I saw her, her face would scream for help. I don't know if it's just me but I always felt she was not happy. There was more to those painful cries. I wanted to know it all. I wanted to know her. I wanted to help her.'

Mahesh stood up and went to the wash basin at the corner of the room. He wet a towel there and came and sat near Kashvi again. He then started wiping her hands and face with the towel. He wiped her lips where food was still stuck from the lunch and also her nose. Then he took out a comb from his pocket and started detangling her hair. I watched him as he did that. Softly and slowly, conscious of not waking her up, he neatened her hair.

'I couldn't meet her for the next few days,' Mahesh said. 'I had work at the other branch of the hospital which is a few miles from here. But throughout the time I was thinking about her. I tried not to, but her face just wouldn't leave my mind. I felt like taking away all her pain.

'When I finally got back, I came to know that she was still not taking her meals properly. I came to meet her and tried to convince her to eat. I thought being her friend might help me to understand her better. After numerous attempts she finally agreed, but with a deal that I would have to buy her a doll. She is smart, you see!' Mahesh said and laughed. He then turned to me and asked, 'When do you hear a twenty-two-year old ask for a doll?' I saw tears in his eyes which he immediately hid and started smiling again.

'She finished her entire meal that day. That was my first step into making her life better and happier. I felt like I have accomplished a lot. I immediately ran to the shop nearby and bought her this.' He picked up the doll lying besideher and said, 'She has named the doll "Sree".' Mahesh showed me the doll with immense happiness and a content smile.

'Since then I would spend most of my time with her whenever I get free from work. I try to fulfil all the wishes she puts up before taking every injection.' Mahesh smiled. 'We had lit lanterns on her birthday and let off dozens of helium balloons. We ate ice creams under a banyan tree and went for boating in the park nearby on a Mickey Mouse boat. We played a lot of pranks on the doctor and the nurses. I was even suspended for a couple of days when the hospital authority came to know that I had sneaked her out of her room at night to the terrace so she could see the stars and the moon in the open sky.' Mahesh giggled and pulled Kashvi's cheeks.

'I have seen her getting better over the years. I know she won't be completely fine but she is happy. I know she can't walk or do things by herself but I also know she would stand by my side. I know she can't console me or cheer me up on days when I would feel low but her eyes are enough to make me feel better,' Mahesh said and then paused suddenly. He was probably trying to control his tears.

'Do you love her?' I asked him.

He smiled and said, 'I don't know if it's love but we do share a very special bond and I want this forever. I want her to be with me forever.'

He then kissed her forehead and said, 'I have a very small house with minimal resources but I'll do anything to keep her happy.'

He looked at her for some time and walked away with tears in his eyes and a smile.

After returning from the hospital, I spent the whole day with myself. Everything that happened was so unbelievable for me. I just couldn't think of a love so unconditional in today's times. It made me question myself and the world we are living in. The more I think about them the more I desire to turn everyone into a Mahesh. He and Kashvi have shown me a really beautiful meaning of love that will stay in my heart forever.

# Garib Rath

## BHASWAR MUKHERJEE

'Suraj beta,' said Colonel Veer Pratap, looking up from the rifle he was cleaning, 'Your nani wishes to visit us this Akshaya Tritiya. She is getting on in her years and I would like you to go to Lucknow and escort her back. This will also give you something to do whilst you await the fate of your applications for your undergraduate studies abroad.'

Suraj, the Colonel's elder son was glued to his newly acquired latest Apple i-Phone—a gift from his doting mother on 'completing school'.

'Hpmf . . . don't even know if the foolish civilian will score enough to get him into a foreign university. And he so desperately needs to get out of India—there is no future here,' the Colonel had grumbled, but knew better than to rebuke his wife.

Reluctantly, Suraj weaned himself away from his toy and gave his father a glassy look. 'Can I drive down in our new

BMW X6?' There would have to be a perk, he felt, in the terrible ordeal his father was subjecting him to.

The Colonel, used to long years of people snapping their heels in attention when he addressed them, felt slighted seeing his gangly, bunched-up son in ill-fitting jeans and tousled hair. 'Smart' phones make people stupid and rob them of their physical well-being as well! he felt.

'Of course, not! It's over hours and Nani will not be able to take the rigours of road travel. Take a flight. Leave on Thursday and return on Saturday. Dismissed.'

'Okay,' sighed Suraj resigned to the fact that his father had the last word in his house.

The firearm in Colonel's hand was a Westley Richards drop-lock double rifle. Despite having retired from the army after an illustrious military career, the passion for guns remained. In a cherry hardwood cabinet next to him was a collection of the world's best firearms—muzzle loaded, breech loaded, carbines and revolvers.

It was rumoured that the cabinet itself was worth a fortune. But then, in the Pratap household, everything reeked of opulence. The family, comprising the Colonel, his wife Sudha and their two sons, lived in the posh Defence Colony in New Delhi in a palatial three-storeyed house with sprawling lawns.

It was rumoured that the Colonel had made his billions by influencing large purchase of defence contracts in the army and was extremely well connected politically. These discussions were, of course, in hushed tones—urban India equates wealth with respectability and hence the family enjoyed immense clout and deference in the city and outside.

As Suraj rose to go to his room, Colonel added, 'Please ensure that you travel economy class while going and business class on return.' Despite his abundant wealth Colonel did not believe in unnecessary expenditure and this discipline had stood him in good stead all his life.

'What! Travel cattle class?' fretted Suraj as he plonked himself at his desk and switched on his laptop. He shared his father's deep dislike for this country and was counting the days when he would fly to beautiful lands afar.

The Colonel's wife Sudha, hearing raised voices, came into the room with a bowl in one hand which contained her work-in-process for the sweetmeats she was preparing for the upcoming ceremony on Monday. The Pratap family had the best cooks in town, but the annual puja was sacrosanct and required the lady of the house to prepare at least one dish as an offering for the gods.

'Why are you screaming at poor Suraj'? she asked, putting more vigour on the batter with her spoon.

'Another bloody civilian!' thought the Colonel. 'You heard me wrong, my dear . . . just too many years in the army I guess,' the Colonel tried to chortle at his own joke. The honey in his voice would have put the sweetness of Sudha's preparations to shame.

'Huh!' snorted Sudha. 'I heard you a mile away in the kitchen. The poor boy will soon be gone. Why are you after his life?'

The Colonel looked up, his voice steeling a little. 'It will be a good experience for him to fend for himself. Perhaps along the way he will grow up.' Looking down and resuming his barrel cleaning, he added under his breath, 'You will then have enough time to devote yourself to spoiling the younger one silly.'

But Sudha had already walked away in a huff.

On Thursday morning at 7 a.m., Suraj stood ready to leave for the airport, while his mother applied vermillion on his forehead and made him sip a spoon of customary curd, believed to augur a safe journey.

Smoking a pipe, the Colonel stood fidgeting next to the Audi Q7 which was to take Suraj to the airport, the air-conditioner and the engine running for a good ten minutes. Concerns of global warming and depletion of fossil fuel reserves clearly did not trouble the Pratap household.

Finally, the Colonel's patience gave up. 'Hurry up for Christ's sake . . . why all this fuss? He's not going to a bloody war, is he?' Then he caught his wife's frosty stare and vented his spleen on the driver. 'And why have you kept the engine running? Bloody waste!' he said and stormed off into the house.

Sudha watched her husband going in and surreptitiously pressed ten thousand rupees into Suraj's hand, 'This is some money for the journey, buy and eat whatever you wish!' she said.

Vivek, the driver, forlornly watched more than half his monthly wages disappear into the depths of Suraj's designer jeans.

Half an hour later, Suraj was dropped off at the Terminal 1D of the New Delhi airport. The flight was thankfully on time and Suraj wrinkled his nose at the people jostling for space and seats in a cramped cabin as the flight was running at full capacity. It reinforced the images in his mind of cattle jostling for space in a pen. 'Cattle class!' he muttered under his breath.

Finding his aisle seat, he settled down, strapped on his seatbelt and plugged his i-Pod headphones to his ear, carving out an isolated world of music from the bedlam around him. He thought about his future, unchartered countries, universities, applications, and apprehensions, and drifted off to sleep.

Suddenly he felt himself being shaken rudely and awoke to panic all around. The elderly lady next to him was praying with her eyes closed, hands folded and mumbling incoherently. The oversized businessman sitting next to the window with a gold chain round his neck was pointing out of the window with his fat fingers, each of which had a ring on it, and telling no one in particular, 'Oh my God! Look! We are doomed!'

A number of passengers from the aisle seats had moved to the emergency row to have a better view from the window. Wisps of black smoke were billowing from under the right wing and the shuddering sound of the propeller was almost drowning the shrieks, cries and shouts inside the aircraft with the passengers in various states of emotional disarray.

Suraj looked at his watch. They had been airborne for about a little over an hour.

For the first time in his life, Suraj felt fear. He felt as if the bottom from his heart had suddenly given way and he was going into free fall. He felt the bile rising and his mouth going dry.

The pilot's voice cut across the maelstrom, 'Ladies and gentlemen, this is your captain speaking. Please return to your seats and put on your seatbelts. We need to make an emergency landing at the Trishul airport in Bareilly. It is the air force's private airport but will allow us in. Please maintain calm to help us make a safe landing.'

Passengers scrambled back to their seats with everyone talking, praying and crying. Air hostesses moved along the aisle with brave smiles on their faces, trying to calm passengers. Their training was being put to test.

Soon, through the still billowing smoke from the right wing, Suraj could see the grass and the ground rushing to meet the aircraft. With a loud thud, the Boeing landed, careened, corrected itself on the rudimentary runway, and came to a shuddering halt. The passengers who till now had been clutching to their arm-rests for dear life, couldn't wait to get off. Soon the aisle was crowded with people pushing and swearing.

As soon as they reached the cool interiors of the terminal building, confusion prevailed, with passengers shouting and jostling around a make-shift enquiry desk, 'Where is our checked-in luggage?'; 'How do we go to Lucknow?'; 'Is a replacement plane coming?'; 'We should sue the airline!'

Suraj, still shaken from the terrifying ordeal, wondered at the human ability to swing from insecurity and fear in one instance to anger and assertiveness in the next.

Despite the trauma of suddenly being yanked from the confines of his sheltered life, Suraj was able to think clearly. He realized that this news would be all over television. He exited the airport building and called home to calm his parents, mainly his hysterical mother, and spurned her offer of a private helicopter pick up. In his own diffident and uncertain way, he was keen to prove to his father that he could handle himself on his own in this world. He explained that he was trying to find alternate transport to Lucknow and asked them to call Nani and explain the situation.

He was able to access the Internet on his phone and decided that his best option would be to travel to the railway station eleven kilometres away and try and get on to the Saharsa Garib Rath which was coming in from Moradabad junction and due to arrive at Bareilly station at 11.30 a.m. If he could catch it, he would be in Lucknow by 5 or 6 p.m. Earlier, Suraj could not have imagined travelling in anything other than an air-conditioned private car, but this choice of transport did not exist. Instinctively, he also debated on whether he had adequate funds for the journey, learning quickly that in a crisis, conservation was the key.

Suraj realized that soon the crowd would come out and try to access the railway and the bus stations. He looked around desperately and found a small gaggle of cycle-rickshaws under a large banyan tree. He walked quickly, now sweating freely under the hot May sun. He supposed that the animated discussion amongst the rickshaw pullers would be on how much to fleece the stranded passengers as this business had landed on their collective laps as manna from heaven.

Suraj did not flinch or bargain when they asked him for a hundred rupees to take him to the railway station and quickly climbed on one, clutching his backpack, thankful that he was travelling light.

The sensibilities of an average upper class Indian are assaulted at the sight of most railway stations and Bareilly station was no exception. At the mercy of erratic train timings, people slept freely on newspapers or otherwise on the floor, oblivious to the heat and the buzzing flies. Suraj was aghast at the sight. He picked his way gingerly to the ticket counter, shuddering at the filth touching his new Nike sneakers.

There was no crowd at the ticket counter, allowing the clerk within the luxury of picking his nose. In the act, he asked Suraj his destination.

Trying to hide his disgust, Suraj asked for an AC first class ticket and the clerk roared with laughter.

'This is India, young man,' he said, wiping sweat with his idle arm, 'I can give you a GC ticket.'

Having no idea what a GC was, Suraj nodded, surprised that it cost him less than a cold coffee. The clerk punched a ticket and tossed it at him with the errant hand. Shuddering, Suraj used the change to cover the ticket. 'Platform 5, coming in ten minutes,' the clerk called behind him, even as Suraj made a dash for it.

Running on the overbridge, Suraj was appalled by the sight of beggars and squalor and saw the train streaming in, as he ran down the steps to the platform.

'Where is the GC?' he shouted to passengers rushing past him. A vendor carrying peeled cucumbers said, 'Follow me!' and Suraj soon found himself sucked into a jampacked compartment with the stench of sweat and urine from the toilets overpowering him.

He felt faint. An elderly couple on seeing him, offered him space and he somehow managed to sit down. They offered him water from a beaten plastic bottle and Suraj had little option but to drink from it. He felt somewhat calmer and soon the swaying coach and the wind rushing in soothed him. He made small conversation with the couple and a young man sitting across, clutching his backpack to his chest all the while.

The quaint sights and sounds of the continuous flow of hawkers soon did not seem oppressive to Suraj any more. He bought some of the cool and freshly peeled cucumber sprinkled with salt from the vendor who had helped him, and it assuaged his hunger a bit. Suraj was learning the art of adaptation quickly.

Suddenly, a blind vendor came into the compartment, selling tops which people allowed him to spin on the floor. As the top spun, it opened out like a flower and lights within flickered accompanied by music.

'Magic tops, magic tops!' roared the vendor as those standing helped him lean against the seat.

'Give it to your child, your elderly father, your nagging wife, or your bored lover! Entertainment for everyone! Rupees thirty, only rupees thirty!' His voice rose full of life, even as his lifeless eyes seemed to roam in every direction trying to detect a buyer for his wares. He was a rotund and dirty man with unkempt hair and an unshaven face. He carried the tops in an open bag slung on his shoulder and felt his way around with a wobbly stick.

A few people took pity and bought a top each. Suraj wondered how a blind man would complete the transaction. What he saw next amazed him.

Those buying gave their money to the blind man. He then reached out to his small pile of currency and held it out for the buyers to enable them pick out the notes, making up the exact change to be returned.

The elderly man saw Suraj's amazement and said, 'They will never cheat him. Have nots do not rob from have nots.'

The blind vendor soon left but returned at an unscheduled stop, crying profusely. He fell down on the dirty compartment floor and used his stick to sweep under the seats. As soon as he finished one seat, he got up and swept the next. A crowd gathered around him as he moved and Suraj could not understand what had happened.

The young man across Suraj who had got up to investigate came back shaking his head, 'Poor fellow cannot find five toys in his bag. He has to give the balance toys and the money to the merchant at Lucknow. Where will this poor fellow get a hundred and fifty rupees from?'

Suraj took out the money and said, 'Please give this to him. Please calm him down.'

In the compartment, the earlier hostile stares changed to one of respect for Suraj. All tried to calm down the vendor, who cried even more and refused to take the money. Finally he relented and fell, clutching Suraj's feet, weeping. Suraj's eyes filled up and he took the man by his shoulders and helped him up, unmindful for the first time of what his hand touched.

The blind vendor left, showering blessings for Suraj and his family. Pulling the chain, he stopped the train and got down.

Suraj sat deep in thought, looking at the vast open fields rushing past outside, even as the sun dipped down bringing to close a very hot day.

At the Hardoi stop, an hour away from Lucknow, there was a sudden commotion. Sweating and panting, the blind vendor burst into the compartment, hurting and cutting himself while trying to get up the steps from the platform. He was smiling and clearly overjoyed. Groping and searching the compartment and asking people, he came to Suraj. In his hand he clutched the hundred and fifty rupees that Suraj had given him. He excitedly narrated that nine compartments ahead, a group of small children had picked up the toys from his open bag. When he went back searching compartment from compartment after getting the money from Suraj, the parents had returned his wares and had apologized for their children's behaviour. He had come back against all odds to return Suraj his money.

Suraj was speechless.

~

After the ceremony and the celebrations on Monday back home, Suraj approached the Colonel.

'Dad,' he said, 'I have decided that I will not go abroad for my undergraduate studies. I wish to stay here.'

When the Colonel furiously tried to protest, Suraj for the first time held up his hand, 'Please hear me out, Father.

I have not shared my experiences of my journey on Garib Rath. And with the wealth that I have earned from that single ride, it seems unfair to call the train Garib Rath—a chariot for the poor.'

Father and son spoke deep into the night.

# Notes on Contributors

**Aaditi Dhyani** belongs to the mountains of Garhwal and lives there with her family. She is currently pursuing BTech in civil engineering and dreaming of becoming an author alongside. Apart from writing, her interests include music, novels and arts.

**Anjali Khurana** is an entertainment professional and a content strategist. She is also a social media buff. Her favourite pastime is to find laughter in the worst tagged YouTube videos. She likes conversations around what the world calls 'impractical'.

**Aparajita Dutta** is a research scholar (MPhil, Jadavpur University) in comparative literature. She writes a blog: www.crystallasia.wordpress.com. She also writes for the football blog GOAlden Times (www.goaldentimes.org). Her stories have been published in various anthologies. She works on gender studies and translation studies and is a member of the non-profit organization, Civilian Welfare Foundation.

**Bhaswar Mukherjee** calls himself an accidental writer and has a number of short stories published in anthologies: *21 Tales to Tell*; *Chronicles of Urban Nomads*; *Something Happened on the Way to Heaven*; and in India's first composite novel *Crossed and Knotted*. After many years as a banker with international banks, Bhaswar now runs his own learning solutions company in Chennai and lives by the maxim 'Carpe Diem' or 'seize the day'.

**Biswas**, carries his family name, **Timshina**, with humility and uses the middle name, **Buddh**, because it sounds fancy. He was born in Gangtok, Sikkim, and is a proud Indian-Nepali. He recently completed civil engineering from Tamil Nadu and writing stories in his answer sheet is what influenced him to become a writer.

**Dalia Jane Saldanha** is a life science student studying in Christ University, Bangalore. She loves using her pen to paint the world with strokes of hope. She aspires to one day integrate her passion for science and arts by becoming a science journalist. Apart from writing poems and short stories, she also enjoys travelling, handcrafting, staging plays, dancing, listening to her best friend on the piano and eating cupcakes. She dreams of growing up and living on a farm with her parents, two brothers, three horses and a turtle.

**Heera Nawaz** is a full-time English teacher at Cambridge School, K.R. Puram, Bangalore. She is also the teacher-coordinator for the *Times of India* for Cambridge School and co-ordinates and organizes all their activities. However, her USP is writing emotional and heartfelt stories on family relationships. She can be reached at heeranawaz@yahoo.com.

**Kamalika Ray,** an ex-banker, is now a freelancer. She has been writing ever since she was a child. An artist at heart, she is passionate about music, painting and photography. Born in Mumbai, she was brought up in Kolkata and later in Ranchi, Jharkhand, and now she is back to her place of birth, Mumbai.

**Krishnasish Jana** is currently pursuing a BTech degree from KIIT University, Bhubaneshwar. Besides writing, he loves to sketch. He is also an avid reader and an active blogger. He lives with his parents at Kharagpur, West Bengal. His poetry blog can be followed at—krishnasishjana.blogspot.in.

A post-graduate in e-business, BSc in chemistry, qualified to be a software engineer, but artist by choice. That's **Madhurie Pandit**. She is a spiritual person who believes in karma and giving back to the society because, 'it is in giving that we receive . . .' Off late, she has started writing down her real life experiences, which she wishes to publish as a book, to inspire people to be kind and humane.

**Prasanthi Pothina** lives in Visakhapatnam, Andhra Pradesh. She studied in Chennai. She is happily married to Satish Kumar, a graphic designer and runs a successful graphic design studio named M&V in Visakhapatnam. They have two children. She has a passion for writing from school days. She has recently published her first book *Life 15: Great Contemporary Short Stories* published by REEM Publications.

**Richa Talukdar** has just passed her 12th board exams from Delhi Public School, Dhaligaon. She was born and brought up in Assam. She started penning diary entries about five to six years ago and instantly fell in love with writing.

**Rupali Tiwari** is a young writer who is currently graduating in homoeopathy. She likes to showcase her feelings with her words. She tries to ensure that her stories are down to earth and have the potential to inspire and influence people anywhere. She has deep interest in writing and reading and currently resides in Chandigarh.

**Sanghamitra Bose** is an 'army brat'. She has spent her early childhood in army cantonments around India before settling down in Baroda. She completed her MBA from M.S. University, Baroda, and embarked on a career spanning hospitality, financial services, academics and the travel industry. She currently lives in Singapore and works for a leading multinational company. A budding author, Sanghamitra also loves travelling, reading and spending time with her little daughter.

**Shaily Bhargava** is an ardent observer, dreamer and a curious soul who enjoys most of her jolly little life in her cocooned dreamland cooking up stories. Her short stories have been published by online literary magazines of repute. She is an equity technical analyst by profession and a freelance writer, photographer and book reviewer by passion. Shaily finds her strength in the 3Cs—coffee, chocolates and Candy Crush.

**Shalini J. Pillai** finds solace in writing. Reading is her first favourite hobby and writing gives her a chance to ponder further over those thoughts. Her biggest dream is to publish her own book. Reading, writing and teaching a language is all she loves and cares to do. Currently, she lives in Mumbai with her husband.

**Shamita Harsh** is a student of journalism at Jamia Millia Islamia and hails from the town of Dehradun. Her debut novel *The Creepy Cuties* was published in January 2014. Ever since then she has authored several short stories and articles. An avid reader and a traveller, Shamita writes narrative fiction, aims to make a career in magazine journalism and fufil her dream of becoming a full-time author.

**Snigdha Khatawkar Mahendra** was born in Nagpur to a Bengali mother and a Maharashtrian father. She is the youngest of their three daughters. Her husband is a practicing surgeon. She has a four-year-old daughter. She writes in her free time.

**Sukanya M.** is an engineer by qualification and works as a teacher for a junior school. She has a deep conviction that a major part of the future is designed in classrooms. She enjoys writing. Her works reflect on everyday experiences that are extraordinary and uncommon. She attempts to converge her aspiration for a better tomorrow and her abilities in all that she does.

**Vijay Kumar** has an MPhil degree in linguistics from Jawaharlal Nehru University. He has worked with advertising and public relations agencies for several years. After which he has been working in the social service sector since in 2002. In 2010, he launched an initiative to bring emotional well-being to orphans and children-at-risk through a curriculum involving art, music and stories. The programme now runs in twenty countries with nine million kids. He used to write a weekly column for *Telegraph*. Currently he is working on his first collection of poems. He lives in Mumbai.

**Dr Yamini Pustake Bhalerao** is a budding author who loves to travel, eat, read and weave stories. Despite being a qualified dentist, a wife and mother, her passion for writing has motivated her to pursue her dream of becoming an author. She maintains a regular blog, The Tea Cup, on eblogger. She is in the process of getting her first novel published and writing her second one.

Also by Ravinder Singh

## I Too Had a Love Story

**Do love stories ever die? . . . How would you react when a beautiful person comes into your life, becomes your most precious possession and then one day goes away from you . . . forever?**

Not all love stories are meant to have a perfect ending. Some stay incomplete, and yet remain beautiful in their own way. *I Too Had a Love Story* is one such saga. It is the tender and heartfelt tale of Ravin and Khushi—two people who found each other on the Internet and fell in love . . . until life put their love to the ultimate test.

Romantic, funny and sincere, this heartbreaking true life story has already touched a million hearts. This bestselling novel is a must-read for anyone who believes in the magic of love . . .

Also by Ravinder Singh

## Can Love Happen Twice?

**When Ravin first said 'I love you . . .' he meant it forever. The world has known this through Ravin's bestselling novel, *I Too Had a Love Story*. But did Ravin's story really end on the last page of that book?**

On Valentine's Day, a radio station in Chandigarh hosts a very special romantic chat show. Ravin and his three best friends are invited as guests to talk about Ravin's love story. But, surprisingly, everyone apart from Ravin turns up. As the show goes live, there is only one question on every listener's mind: what has happened to Ravin?

To answer this question the three friends begin reading from a handwritten copy of Ravin's incomplete second book— the entire city listens breathlessly, unable to believe the revelations that follow.

This highly anticipated sequel by Ravinder Singh is an emotional rollercoaster that bravely explores the highs and lows of love.

Also by Ravinder Singh

# *Love Stories That Touched My Heart*

***Love*—only a four-letter word, yet it's so powerful that it can conquer anything in this world!**

We've all experienced the first flush of love and remember the lingering fragrance of it. For ages, love has remained one of the most cherished experiences that everyone wishes to live through at least once. Humanity, time and again, has coined many definitions to describe this beautiful emotion, but this small word is a feeling that can't simply be defined. It has to be narrated . . . in the form of stories—love stories.

*Love Stories That Touched My Heart* is a collection of such stories from readers who have a tale to tell; stories that they would like to share.

Selected and edited by Ravinder Singh, this anthology—made up of the stories that touched Ravin's heart the most—will make you believe that someone, somewhere, is made for you.

Also by Ravinder Singh

## *Your Dreams Are Mine Now*

**'It can't be love . . .' he thinks and immediately his heart protests.**

They are complete opposites!

She's a small-town girl who takes admission in Delhi University (DU). An idealist, studies are her first priority.

He's a Delhi guy, seriously into youth politics in DU. He fights to make his way. Student union elections are his first priority.

But then opposites attract as well!

A scandal on campus brings them together, they begin to walk the same path and somewhere along, fall in love . . . But their fight against evil comes at a heavy price, which becomes the ultimate test of their lives.

Against the backdrop of dominant campus politics, *Your Dreams Are Mine Now* is an innocent love story that will tug at your heartstrings.

Also by Ravinder Singh

## *Like It Happened Yesterday*

**Has anyone ever asked you—what were the best days of your life?**

That one period of your life you always wanted to go back to? And live that life . . . one more time?

When asked this, I closed my eyes and went back in my own past. And I thought . . .

. . . of the days, when life's most complex choices had a simple solution of *Akkad Bakkad Bambey Bo*!
. . . of the seasons when rains were celebrated by making paper boats.
. . . of the times when waiting at the railway crossing meant counting the bogies of the train passing by.

When I opened my eyes, it seems Like it Happened Yesterday! Like it was yesterday that I broke my first tooth and fell in love for the first time. Like it was yesterday, when I was about to lose my friend, and suddenly he became my best friend.

I look back and it becomes a journey full of adventure. It makes me laugh, it makes me cry and I know I'm here because I was . . .

Come, hold my hand, and take this trip with me. It will be yesterday for you, once again!